George Granville

Recollections of Arthur Penrhyn Stanley, Late Dean of Westminster. Three Lectures Delivered in Edinburgh in November, 1882

George Granville Bradley

Recollections of Arthur Penrhyn Stanley, Late Dean of Westminster. Three Lectures Delivered in Edinburgh in November, 1882

Reprint of the original, first published in 1883.

1st Edition 2024 | ISBN: 978-3-38533-185-3

Verlag (Publisher): Outlook Verlag GmbH, Zeilweg 44, 60439 Frankfurt, Deutschland
Vertretungsberechtigt (Authorized to represent): E. Roepke, Zeilweg 44, 60439 Frankfurt, Deutschland
Druck (Print): Books on Demand GmbH, In de Tarpen 42, 22848 Norderstedt, Deutschland

RECOLLECTION

OF

ARTHUR PENRHYN STANLEY

LATE DEAN OF WESTMINSTER

Three Lectures

DELIVERED IN EDINBURGH IN NOVEMBER 1882

BY

GEORGE GRANVILLE BRADLEY D.D.

DEAN OF WESTMINSTER
HONORARY FELLOW OF UNIVERSITY COLLEGE OXFORD

NEW YORK

CHARLES SCRIBNER'S SONS

1883

INTRODUCTION.

THE following pages are the result of an attempt to comply with a request made on behalf of the Philosophical Institution of Edinburgh. The Directors did me the honour of expressing a wish that I should open their winter session by delivering two lectures on my much lamented friend and predecessor, the late Dean of Westminster. I could not refuse to avail myself of such an opportunity for placing on record my recollections of one to whose intimacy I had been admitted in early youth, and whose friendship I had been privileged to enjoy for more than forty years. I felt it, however, due alike to the memory of my friend, and to the legitimate claims of those whom I was to address, to bring before them something more than mere personal reminiscences of one who had filled so large a space in the literary and theological history of the whole period during which I had known him. I thought it right, therefore, to prepare myself for the task by a careful re-perusal of his published works, especially of the numerous lectures, pamphlets, articles, essays, and occasional sermons which, even more markedly than his longer and more elaborate works, bear the true impress of his mind and character. Not a few of these which had escaped my memory or notice were placed at my disposal by various friends; and in addition to all that I had preserved of my own correspondence, I was permitted to avail myself of letters, and notes of personal recollections, entrusted to me by the kindness of some who had been bound to him by the closest ties of enduring friendship. It soon became apparent that the materials placed in my hands, though insignificant in comparison with those which were being gradually collected with a view to more detailed memoirs, could scarcely be adequately dealt with in the compass of two evening lectures, even before so kind and forbearing an audience as I was prepared to find in the city of Edinburgh. Arrangements were very kindly made for the delivery of a third lecture — let me thank my friends there for its cordial reception — at Fettes College; and thus with some necessary curtailment the greater portion of the following pages was spoken as printed. I have not thought it necessary to indicate the paragraphs which, out of consideration for the time and patience of singularly attentive and sympathetic listeners, were omitted in the actual delivery of the lectures. As, however, the greater portion of the matter devoted to Dean Stanley's earlier life, at Alderley, Rugby, and Oxford, formed the subject not of the first but of the second lecture, that which was given at Fettes College, I have thought it better to arrange what is now printed in three consecutive chapters. I have thus preserved the order in which all that I had prepared was actually written, as well as that which will be most convenient to the general reader. But I have retained throughout the form, and, with a few necessary corrections, the actual words of the lectures as actually delivered. They were delivered, it will be remembered, in Scotland, and before a Scottish audience; and I therefore felt myself warranted in dwelling with a not unreasonable emphasis on the singularly close ties which united him of whom I spoke to the sympathies and affections of those whom I was addressing.

I need hardly add that the subject on which I spoke was one of exceeding interest to myself.

Those who are at the pains of glancing at the following pages will see that I disclaimed from the very first any attempt to speak of Arthur Stanley otherwise than as a deeply attached and grateful friend, and as one who largely sympathised with his views. Had I not done so I should have written differently, or not at all. I trust, however, that I have not allowed my warm affection for one who was, for many years of his life, engaged in almost ceaseless controversies, to cause me to give needless pain to those whose difference of views on some most important subjects made them unable to share the feelings with which he was regarded by those who were more or less in sympathy with him. I should regret any want of fairness on my own part as in itself blamable. I should regret it the more, as some of those who were necessarily brought in the course of many controversies into the most direct collision with my dear friend, have spoken with generous warmth and tenderness of one, the beauty of whose character they could recognise without undervaluing their disagreement with his opinions, sentiments, or language.

I feel, however, that in saying even this, I am attaching an undue importance to the publication of what can have no claim to more than a passing and fugitive interest. Nothing could be further from my purpose than to offer this most imperfect sketch as in any way a substitute for, or even an instalment of, a biography of Arthur Stanley. Great as was the kindness of his literary executors and personal friends, it was impossible for me to avail myself of more than a small fraction of the documents and papers which, owing to his own habits and the prescient care of so many to whom he was dear, are assuming proportions of almost unexampled abundance. Yet I venture to hope that the publication even of the short summary of his life and work which is comprised in these three chapters, may be not unwelcome to some at least among the many who, beyond the limits of those to whom they were directly addressed, had yet felt the spell of his character, or had been attracted or instructed by his writings.

I may conclude with a warm expression of my gratitude to those of his friends who have kindly allowed me the use in some cases of their own correspondence, in others of their notes of personal reminiscences. I ought especially to name Dr. Greenhill, Professor Max Müller, Rev. W. B. Philpot, Rev. H. H. Montgomery, Mr. Victor Williamson, and Mr. John Hodgkin;

above all my thanks are due to his two surviving literary executors, Mr. Theodore Walrond and Mr. George Grove, not only for their ready acquiescence in the present publication, but for the invaluable assistance which in various forms I received from each of them.

DEANERY, WESTMINSTER,
December 31, 1882.

CONTENTS.

CHAPTER I.

CHAPTER II.

(From 1840 to 1863.)

OXFORD — CANTERBURY — OXFORD.

FELLOW OF UNIVERSITY COLLEGE, OXFORD, 1840-50.

CANON OF CANTERBURY, 1851-1858.

CHAPTER III.

(From 1863 to 1881.)

WESTMINSTER.

RECOLLECTIONS

OF

ARTHUR PENRHYN STANLEY

RECOLLECTIONS

OF

ARTHUR PENRHYN STANLEY.

CHAPTER I.

(From his Birth in 1815 to 1840.)

ALDERLEY — RUGBY — OXFORD.

YOUR directors have called on me to undertake a very interesting, but by no means an easy task. Some months have passed since they requested me to speak to you here of one whose face and voice will long be remembered among you, my own dear friend — may I not say yours also? — the late Dean of Westminster. Flattering as I felt their proposal to be, I shrank with unfeigned reluctance from accepting it. In default of leisure, and in the absence, the comparative absence, of necessary materials and documents, I despaired of doing any adequate justice to his memory, or of satisfying the claims which a Philosophical Society in — I use his own words — "this great and historic centre of Scottish life," might justly make in behalf of one of such rare and surpassing gifts, whose life was so closely bound up with the religious and literary history of the last forty years. But I was

encouraged to believe that I might look for a sympathetic and forbearing audience; and I was given to
understand that there was a general wish that he who
should attempt to recall him to you should be none
other than his successor in the post to which his own
genius had added so much exceptional significance.
To that wish I deferred, and am here to-day to fulfil
my engagement, or to attempt to do so to the utmost
of my powers.

Let me say at once that I would gladly have
brought before you a sketch of each of what I may
venture to call the seven distinct and marked stages
of his life. They are, first, his childhood in his home
at Alderley; next, his boyhood at Rugby, where
he grew up under the influence of his great teacher,
Dr. Arnold. Then follows his brilliant career as a
scholar of Balliol. Then, fourthly, the many important years that he passed as a resident Member
of the University of Oxford, and as an active and
influential Tutor, no longer of Balliol, but of University College. After this come the seven quiet years
of his Canonry at Canterbury; then his work as
Professor of Ecclesiastical History at Oxford; and,
finally, the closing and culminating stage of all, his
life and death as Dean of Westminster.

It would, however, be obviously impossible to bring
before you in any detail all these chapters in his life,
though each has a peculiar character and a special
interest of its own. Nor can anything be more
remote from my present purpose than any attempt

to forestall his future biographer; and I shall pass
over without notice many of the most important
passages in his career, only attempting any fulness
of detail, where my own recollections, or the special
circumstances of those whom I address, or other
sufficient reasons, guide me to do so. If I have made
a wrong choice in my selection, you will forgive me.
I must take comfort in the hope that you have come
here not so much to criticise the literary merits or
the judgment of your Lecturer, as to renew your
acquaintance with his friend.

To that friend I stand too near in affection — I am
bound to him too closely by enduring ties of sympathy
and gratitude — to play the part of a censor or a
critic.   I cannot stand aside, and look at him, or speak
of him, as a stranger would.   This you will not expect
or wish.   But I can promise that I will not willingly
misrepresent him by a hair's breadth, or paint him for
one moment other than he was; other than I have
known him in constant intercourse since I won his
friendship as I passed from boyhood.   In life "he
feared no man's rebuke;" and we, his friends — I, for
one — feel no need to speak of him with bated breath,
or in apologetic accents.   I will simply try to do in
short compass what his biographer will do, we all
trust, on a larger scale; to set before you Arthur
Stanley as he lived and as he died; himself, and no
other — his real character, his real self; and, if I
venture to add something as to his views on the most
important of all subjects, I will leave him, so far as

possible, to speak for himself. Great as was his consideration for others, unbounded as was his tolerance, large and tender as were his sympathies, there never breathed a more outspoken, a more fearless soul, or a more transparent expounder of all that lay next his heart.

And I assure myself that I may do this with an especial trustfulness before a Scottish audience. You knew the man, and he you. Nowhere did he more freely open all the secrets of that seething brain, and that ardent temperament — that *perfervidum ingenium* which is no monopoly of the countrymen of Buchanan. To Scotsmen here, to Scotsmen at St. Andrews, he spoke in his later years with a fulness of confidence not exceeded in his letters to his dearest friends, or by all that he uttered when his soul was stirred within him by that long delayed visit to the new England beyond the seas. Reared and educated in England, he was unknown among you till some few years after the publication of his " Life of Arnold " had lifted his name above the level of a merely academical reputation. I have mislaid, alas! but I well remember, the letter in which, 34 years ago, on his first visit to the Scottish home of Principal Shairp, the present Professor of Poetry in my own University, with the recollection of his winter in Greece still unfaded in his memory, he spoke of Edinburgh as an Athens — as (forgive me the quotation) a "coarser Athens" — and described the kindness with which he was everywhere received as the Biographer of Arnold, the interest

evinced in one in whom Scotsmen saw, and the words
on his lips had a deep significance, *Elisha the son of
Shaphat, who poured water on the hands of Elijah.*
A year passed, and he came to Scotland on a sadder
errand — to close his father's eyes; even as, twice
later, he came to lay in their ancestral grave the two
brothers of her whom he married. But long before
his marriage had bound him by a closer tie to these
northern regions, Scotland had laid upon him the spell
which she maintained to the very end. In repeated
snatches of autumnal leisure as Tutor at Oxford, as
Canon of Canterbury, he had visited, often under the
guidance of the friend whom I have already named,
one after another of the scenes, rich in legendary or
poetic or religious or historic interest, with which
Scotland abounds. As time went on, it is not too
much to say that no native of Scotland could be more
imbued, more saturated, with all the manifold associations of Scottish story or history, "the most
romantic," as he would vehemently assert, "by far
of all European histories," than one who never drew
a breath of Scottish air till he had become famous
by writing the life of one of the most typical of Englishmen.

Thus on the very first occasion that he opened his
lips to lecture on Ecclesiastical History at Oxford,
years before family ties had made him almost a countryman of your own, in urging on his future pupils
the importance of including among the original records of history "monuments, and grave-stones, and

epitaphs on the very spots where they lie;" "the
mountain, and the stream, and the shapeless stone,
that has survived even history and tradition," he
chose the first of two examples from "the caves, the
moors, and moss-bogs of the Western Lowlands;"
from "the rude grave-stones," with their savage
rhymes and texts and names that are to be found
from shore to shore of the Scottish kingdom. And
he placed these side by side with "the faded paint-
ings, the broken sculptures, the rude epitaphs, that
lie underground in the Roman catacombs."

It is rarely that he attempts to describe Scottish
scenery as scenery; Nature, indeed, as Nature, he
seldom, I might say never, allowed himself to paint.
But he loved to dwell on his enjoyment of the scenery
of St. Andrews; "the roar and expanse of the sea on
one side, the shattered relics of the Cathedral on the
other"— the "two voices," as he would call them,
"each a mighty voice." Of all the great names of literature none was so dear to him as that of Walter Scott,
that "second Shakespeare of your own," the "spell
and glamour" of whose "wizard notes" he felt at
threescore as strongly as he had felt them in boyhood;
of whom he delighted to speak not in Scotland only,
but alike on the sacred soil of Palestine and in his
own Abbey, now as the greatest and purest writer of
fiction, now as "one of the greatest religious teachers
of Scottish Christendom." Later in life he could no
more visit Tours without reading and re-reading for
the fiftieth time, as he said, "Quentin Durward," than

he could have made a pilgrimage to the graves of
the Covenanters without once more renewing his acquaintance with "Old Mortality." Behind "all the
wretchedness of life, and all the levity of language"
which marred the genius of "the prodigal son of the
Scottish Church," he could find in Robert Burns not
"the poet only, but the prophet;" in that "wise
humour, that sagacious penetration, that tender pathos," he could find at times fragments of a teaching
that breathes the spirit, "not of this or that Confession, but of the Sermon on the Mount." On his
undying interest in the religious history of Scotland
I need hardly dwell, or remind you how keenly he
appreciated not only the more romantic and attractive features of its earlier chapters, but "the defi-
ant self-reliance and dogged resistance to superior
power," "the force of unyielding conviction," "the
indomitable native vigour," "the marvellous energy,"
which, with whatever drawbacks — drawbacks on
which he spoke to you with entire and characteristic
frankness — marked its later developments. How gallantly did he meet the charges brought against the
clergy of Scotland, at one time by Samuel Johnson,
at a more recent period by Mr. Buckle. Even Milton's sneer at Rutherford he meets by the one method
which he was never tired of commending to others,
of practising himself — by bringing out the equally
true, the more touching, the more Christian side of
the stern yet affectionate Pastor of Anworth. With
what delight did he dwell "on the divine fire of

Scotland's Burning Bush that lies hid beneath the
rough husk" of logical subtleties and stubborn protests, of testimonies and confessions. You know how
his soul yearned over the combination of deep religious sentiment, " of a sanctity equal to that of the
strictest Covenanter or the strictest Episcopalian,"
with " a just and philosophic moderation," the crown-
ing instance of which he found in Robert Leighton,
"the most apostolical," as he deliberately called him,
"of all protestant Scotsmen;" who held a place in
his affection and veneration side by side with, if not
even above, that held by Richard Baxter in the South.
You may have smiled as he rebuked in his own manner the eccentricities or the shortcomings or the ex-
cesses of this or that form of Scottish Christianity;
for you knew that your Church and people had no
more devoted or more earnest champion; that all
that was great and noble and inspiring in its past or
present history was as dear to him as it was to you.
Some of you can remember the delight with which
(not here only, but in Oxford) he called up from the
recollections of his earlier days his one interview,
the first and last, " ending in front of the academic
church at Oxford," with the "wise and good" Dr.
Chalmers. With what fervour did he recite, not here
only, but at Westminster, the burning words in which
Thomas Carlyle poured out his angry but noble
grief over the open grave of your Edward Irving.
How he rejoiced heart and soul in the society of Nor-
man M'Leod; how in Erskine of Linlathen he found

one "to hold brief converse with whom was to have his conversation in heaven." The very last literary work on which that brain, active to the last, was ever engaged, was a paper on the Westminster Confession, the proofs actually corrected in that fatal illness which took him away from the great work that he was doing, beneath the very roof where that "venerable document," as he loved to call it, first saw the light.

I say nothing of Scottish friends and companions and fellow workers who gathered round him from Oxford days to the day on which he breathed his last; nothing of that Scottish lady whose name will be inseparably connected with his own, in whose grave he lies. I have said enough to remind you, were it needed, that he of whom I am to speak was one towards whom Scotland may feel as the almost adopted son of her own soil, almost bone of your bone, flesh of your flesh.

Let me pass at once to the story of his life.

He was born on December 13, in the eventful year 1815. The place of his birth was Alderley, in Cheshire, of which his father was rector, a place which for many centuries had formed part of the ancestral estates of the great house of Stanley. Of a branch of that house, not ennobled till the next generation, his uncle, Sir John Stanley, who lived at the Park hard by, was the representative and head.

On the position which the family of Stanley has held in English history, whether in the Tudor or Stuart reigns, or later on, it is not necessary to enlarge. The thoughts of a resident in Westminster will naturally turn to the Stanley who on the field of Bosworth placed on the head of the first Tudor king, his own stepson, the crown that is so often reproduced, sometimes with the bush on which it was found hanging, in the stately chapel of Henry VII. It is possible that the memory of those to whom he speaks may travel rather to the fatal field of Flodden, where the sword of a Stanley of the next generation drank so deeply of the best blood of Scotland. Scotsmen and Englishmen will alike be interested to note the one and only passage in which one scion of that race cared publicly to recall his lineage. It is that in which, after describing the marvellous promise of Alexander Stuart, the shortlived son of James IV., the pupil of Erasmus, of "gentle manners, playful humour, keen as a hound in the pursuit of knowledge" — Ah! you see why I dwell on the words — "the young Marcellus," as he calls him, "of the Scottish Church," "if," he goes on to say, "he fell in the memorable charge of my namesake on that fatal day, may he accept, thus late, the lament which a kinsman of his foe would fain pour over his untimely bier."

For a charming picture of the home of Arthur Stanley's infancy and boyhood, his friends owe a debt of gratitude to Mr. Augustus Hare. "Few country places," he says, "in England possess such a singular charm as Alderley:" and he goes on, in an article in Macmillan's Magazine for September in last year, to describe the spot "where the flat pasture

lands of Cheshire rise suddenly into the rocky ridge
of Alderley Edge, with the Holy Well under an
overhanging cliff; its gnarled pine trees, its storm-
beaten beacon tower, ready to give notice of an inva-
sion, and looking far over the green plain to the smoke
which indicates in the horizon the presence of great
manufacturing towns." He tells us how the beautiful
beech woods, which clothe the western side of that
upheaving ridge, feather down over mossy lawns to
the lake or "mere" beneath. I wish that time allowed
me to read to you a description of the scene written
by Arthur Stanley's mother at the age of eighteen, in
the first few months of her married life. You will find
it in the Memorials of his two parents published by
himself on the anniversary of her death, in 1879.
You would agree with me that for clearness and delicacy of touch, that gifted son could hardly have surpassed it in the full maturity of his powers. The
Rectory itself cannot be described better than in Mr.
Hare's words. "A low house, with a veranda forming
a wide balcony for the upper storey, where bird-cages
hung among the roses; its rooms and passages filled with
pictures, books, and old carved oak furniture." His father, in his "Familiar History of British Birds," speaks
of watching the starlings "on a well-mown, short-
grassed lawn, within a stone's throw of which stands an
ivy-mantled parish church, with its massy grey tower,
from the turreted pinnacle of which rises a tall flagstaff,
crowned by a weather-cock." You will, I think, forgive
me for entering into these details in speaking of one
to whom all such associations were so peculiarly dear.

Of his father he has himself left us a picture in his
Memoirs of Bishop Stanley, and in the work which I
have just mentioned. His personal character and his
position in the Church of England were so peculiar
and so striking, and their bearing on his son's career,
however difficult to estimate precisely, were so undeniable, that, quite apart from their intrinsic interest,
I must not pass them by. His educational advantages
in early life were scanty. He did his best to compensate for their absence by untiring industry at Cambridge. He attained considerable proficiency and
academic honours in mathematics, a study in which
his son was so unversed, that at least after the close
of his school life, an arithmetical sum was to him an
almost insoluble problem.* Active on foot, and one
of the very first forerunners of modern Alpine climb-
ers, as much at home in the saddle as his son was the
reverse, he never hunted or joined in field sports. But
the people of Alderley long remembered the courage
with which, while all his respectable parishioners stood
aghast at his temerity, that true son of a gallant house
darted on his little black horse into the midst of a
riotous crowd, and by his mere appearance stopped a
desperate prize fight. As keen an observer of outward
nature as his son's friend, Charles Kingsley, he was the
author of a "Familiar History of Birds," which, thanks
to its accurate and careful studies of animal life, may
outlive many graver scientific works. But the father

* "Were I," he once said late in life, "a citizen of this (American)
State," — it was one in which an educational test was enforced, —
"I should never enjoy the franchise."

of Arthur Stanley was far more than this. He was
not only a liberal clergyman at a time when to hold
liberal views was, at all events so far as the rural clergy
were concerned, almost to court social isolation : he
was an indefatigable and apostolic priest at a time
when and in a district where the standard of clerical
work was still deplorably low. In moral courage he
was not surpassed by his fearless son. He was almost
the first parochial clergyman of the Church of England
to do his utmost to advocate and to promote the spread
of general as well as of religious instruction among
the neglected agricultural population. He was almost
if not quite the first parochial clergyman who ventured
to lecture before a Mechanics' Institute on the then
young and suspected science of Geology. In the midst
of the alarm and panic of 1829 he attempted to throw
oil on the troubled waters by publishing "A Few Words
in behalf of our Catholic Brethren." In the crisis of
the Reform Agitation in 1831, when the very word
"Reform" was a sound of terror to the mass of the
clergy, he had won sufficient influence to persuade
a group of clergymen in his diocese to join him in a
petition to Parliament for the removal of some of the
most undeniable of the abuses then existing in the
English Church — a petition which the excellent
Bishop of his diocese at once declined to present.

Removed in 1837 to the see of Norwich, he was
grudgingly received in his new sphere, a diocese in
which the clergy were perhaps even more than elsewhere indisposed to welcome a Whig Bishop, the

nominee of a Whig Premier, who had vainly urged on
a cautious Primate the name of Thomas Arnold as the
preacher at his consecration. In his very first sermon
he raised a whirlwind of opposition by speaking of the
duty of forbearance towards Dissent, and of the importance of imparting secular as well as religious education in parochial schools. But this was only the first
of a series of shocks which, in the midst of entire and
absolute devotion to the spiritual and moral welfare
of his huge diocese, he inflicted on the public opinion
of his own clergy, and of wider circles. Both as a
Clergyman and as a Bishop he was emphatically before his time. As we look back at his career we see
him now standing on a platform at Norwich side by
side with an Irish Catholic priest, Father Mathew,
the Apostle in the sister island of the cause of tem-
perance ; now advocating in the National Society
such modifications of school teaching as would open
the school-doors to the children of Non-conformists ;
now addressing a reluctant House of Lords and two
indignant Archbishops in favour of relaxing the terms
of subscription then enforced on the English clergy ;
now, in a sermon which was at once characterised
as the boldest ever preached in St. Paul's Cathedral,
disavowing in the presence of the Metropolitan Clergy
and their Bishop, the doctrine as usually understood of
the Apostolical succession ; now, strange and almost
incredible as it may sound to you, censured by a certain section of the religious public for welcoming to the
hearth and to the heart of his episcopal home one so

honoured in all circles as the gifted lady who then bore
the name of Jenny Lind. If he was the first English
Bishop of his day to throw himself heart and soul, in
conjunction with the present Earl of Shaftesbury, into
the movement for the establishment of Ragged Schools,
he was, no doubt, the very first of English Bishops to
preach in his own Cathedral a funeral sermon in honour
of a saintly Quaker. We live in an age of transition.
It is already difficult to understand, still more to make
due allowance for, the storms of obloquy and clamour
which one after another of such proceedings awoke
in large and influential circles. They at times even
exceeded those which his son encountered years after
with hereditary fearlessness. But if they did much to
embitter the life and impair the usefulness of one of the
most devoted of God's servants who ever held the high
office of an English Bishop, it is encouraging to remember how steadily and increasingly he won his way to the
respect and affection of those who most differed from
him, of some of those who had expressed that difference
most strongly. When, during a rare visit to Scotland
at the close of twelve years of unwearied episcopal
work, he was called away after a short illness under the
hospitable roof of Brahan Castle, there was a general
and frank recognition of what was lost, and a genuine
burst of sorrow throughout all East Anglia. Clergy
and Laity, Churchmen and Dissenters, adults and
children, mourned alike for one who " had found his
diocese a wilderness and left it in comparison a cultivated field," whose "good grey hairs and elastic step,

and open countenance, with its striking profile and quick searching glances," are still affectionately remembered among Norfolk parsonages and in poor men's dwellings. His funeral at Norwich drew together a concourse like in numbers and in the diversity of its elements to that which gathered last year round another grave in the Abbey of Westminster. At that sight " there came across me," said his son, " as it had never come before, the high ideal and the great opportunities of the life of an English Bishop." And if there was much in the son which he did not inherit from his father, and if some of the father's gifts were not transmitted to his son, yet I feel that the son would have forbidden me to speak to you of himself without reminding you of what he owed to a father whom he never mentioned without honour and reverence.

Of his mother also he has drawn his own portrait. But he knew well that no words could describe the debt he owed to her. She was indeed the ideal mother for such a son. Quiet, calm, thoughtful, dignified even in early womanhood (she became a wife at eighteen): deeply religious, "with a spiritual insight which belonged to that larger sphere of religion which is above and beyond the passing controversies of the day;" observant, and somewhat reticent, yet full of sympathy to those whom she loved, she possessed in girlhood and retained to the end "a rare delicacy of intelligence," which Sydney Smith happily characterised as " *a porcelain understanding*," together with a literary taste and power of expression of which few but her

children were aware till the publication of her Memorials. She watched with trembling and aided with
wisdom the early development of the gifted nature
of her second son, whose rare genius she quickly rec-
ognized, and whose delicate frame and unformed constitution she did her best, with a mother's devotion,
to consolidate and strengthen. And the son, as he
grew up, repaid that devotion, so far as such debts
can be repaid, sevenfold into her bosom. Every year
of her long life she became increasingly dear to him;
every year her "firm faith, calm wisdom, and tender
sympathy, speaking the truth in love, counselled,
encouraged, and comforted" him who inscribed these
words upon her tombstone. When death had taken
from her almost at a stroke the husband of her youth,
and two sons whose bones "lie severed far and wide,"
the one survivor drew her more and more closely to
his filial and loving heart.

It was in such a home, and with such parents, that
five children passed their childhood and opening life :
Owen, who inherited his father's taste for the sea, and
chose it for his calling ; Mary, whose active life spent
in works of beneficence at Norwich, among the soldiers
on the Bosphorus, and in Westminster, will not lightly
be forgotten ; Arthur, of whom I am speaking ;
Charles, the future Royal Engineer and Secretary to
the Governor of Van Diemen's Land ; and the one
sister who still survives to bear, as the wife of the
Master of the Temple and Dean of Llandaff, a name
honoured greatly in the English Church.

The future biographer may supplement Mr. Hare's picture of that home; he can hardly improve upon it. It is interesting to dwell on it as one of the very highest types of that large class of cultivated, modest, and well-ordered family circles, which have so often grown up under the quiet roof of English parsonages and Scottish manses, and which have made the sons of the clergy so important an element in our own, and, indeed, in all Protestant countries; and I cannot help reminding you how, towards the very close of his life, in a sermon preached at Glasgow, after enlarging " on the sacred and beneficent institution of a married clergy," Arthur Stanley spoke of his own memory of " a happy and peaceful childhood spent under the shade of the tower of a parish church, and under the roof of a parish parsonage, still," he said, " after all the vicissitudes of a chequered life, familiar, dear, and sacred beyond any other spot on the surface of the earth."

I shall follow Mr. Hare's guidance for a short time longer. The mother's letters bring before us her second boy as frail and delicate, yet beginning, when infancy was over, " to expand as one of the spring flowers in Alderley May time," and, again, as " talking incessantly, full of pretty speeches, repartees, and intelligence;" " like his elder brother," the gallan sailor that was to be, " but softer and more affectionate;" sorely divided between fear and curiosity (that curiosity which never died) at the entrance of the enchanted cave of the neighbourhood; revelling in all the legends of the countryside; at five years old devouring Miss Edgeworth's "Frank," and translating its lessons into practical life ; living already in a little world of books and poetry of his own.

At eight years old a growing shyness and silence alarmed his parents, who were wise enough greatly to dread too exclusive an activity of brain and nerve, and it was resolved to try the effect of a transference to a small and homelike school near the seaside. There we are allowed to see "the little sylph," as his aunt calls him, happy in his own way, proud, like other little boys, of hearing himself called by his surname of Stanley, prouder of bringing home a prize-book — the first of many — for history, devouring " Madoc " and " Thalaba," and forming a love which he was always eager to avow for Southey's now much forgotten poetry ; laying the foundation of his wonderful faculty for letter writing by writing home long histories of school life, describing his drill sergeant "as telling him to put on a bold, swaggering air, and not to look sheepish;" astonishing every one when he came home by his memory and his quickness in picking up knowledge ; yet disquieting his mother more than ever, when his twelfth birthday was passed, by having no other pursuits, nor anything he cares for, except reading; "often," she says, " I am sure, very unhappy, with a laudable desire to be with other boys, yet when with them finding his incapacity to enter into their pleasures." " Ah ! " she says, with a cry almost of despair, " it is so difficult to manage Arthur. Yet after all I suspect," she adds, with rare sagacity and prophetic instinct, " I suspect that this is Arthur's worst time, and that he will be a happier man than he is a boy." Yet even she hardly foresaw the unrevealed wealth of social gifts, of unbounded cheerfulness and merriment, of power of adapting himself to the most varied circles, above all, the inexhaustible capacity for tender friendship, that lay latent under that passing cloud of boyish shyness and reserve.

It is rarely that the general public need be called on to pore over the faded records of the childhood of distinguished men. But there is a oneness in the development of Arthur Stanley's mind that gives a singular interest to even his boyish, to even his childish, effusions. No doubt that young brain was at this time abnormally active. There lay before me, as I wrote what I now say, a small MS. volume, written, from beginning to end, in a boyish but, strange as it may seem to those who knew him later, a singularly clear hand. On the title-page are inscribed the words, " The Poetical Works of Arthur Penrhyn Stanley, Vol. II.," and underneath is a drawing, his own handiwork, of Neptune in his Chariot, with Amphitrite and the sea nymphs sporting around. The volume contains 13 or 14 poems in various metres, and on various subjects; not only odes to the Humming-bird, to the Owl, to the Stork, but to such abstract ideas as Superstition, to Time, to Forgiveness, to Death, to Sleep, to Justice. It includes a poem on the Destruction of the Druids, written in a tripping dactylic metre, and a ballad on a strange legend of

King Harold. This, remember, is Vol. II., and the
poems, which are carefully dated, were written in the
years 1826–27, when the young poet was of the age
of 10 and 11. They seem to me (I will not trouble you
with specimens) to show more marked originality than
almost any, that I have seen, of his English verses
written much later at Rugby. His little study there
soon gained the nickname of " Poet's Corner," and from
time to time he gained much credit by his school com-
positions in English verse, especially for a prize poem,
composed at the age of 18, on Charles Martel's victory
near Tours, "the more than Marathon of France," as he
happily calls it in his final line. Yet I suspect that, quite
apart from the effect of public-school life on a boy of
poetic temperament, his Rugby life developed mainly
other sides of that imaginative and active brain. He
was intent there rather on absorbing ideas and knowledge than on giving out his own impressions. Certainly
in my own day it was not so much to him as to Arthur
Hugh Clough — the gifted author of much besides,
known perhaps to some here through that charming
description of a Long Vacation spent by Oxford
undergraduates at the Bothie with the name un-
pronounceable to Southern lips — that we Rugby
schoolboys looked back as the true poet among our
distinguished predecessors.

The year 1828 was an eventful epoch in Arthur
Stanley's life. It was the year marked by the first
foreign tour of one who was afterwards to be a traveller
of travellers. Mr. Hare has told us how when first he

saw the great *Pic du Midi* rise above a mass of clouds, he could find no words to express his ecstasy but " What shall I do ? what shall I do ? " And his journal written at the time was worthy of the future author of "Sinai and Palestine." I have been favoured with words written in November of the same year by a discerning lady, an absolute stranger to the Stanley family, in which she speaks of herself as having been —

"Much pleased and still more surprised by the perusal of a journal during a tour in the Pyrenees made in the last summer by an English family. The writer is a boy of twelve years old, who, if he attains manhood, and keeps the promise he has hitherto given, will, I do not doubt, hereafter be classed amongst the distinguished literary characters of this country. His mind appears to have been open to all the beauty and wonders he saw, which he describes in language always good, and often poetical. The account he gives of their expedition to the ' Maladetta ' is one of the very best I ever read of similar excursions in *any* book of travels."

Such prophecies may have been often made. It is seldom that they meet with such entire fulfilment !

It was in the same year that, after much consultation, his parents resolved to remove their boy to Rugby, and place him under the care of Dr. Arnold, who was just entering on a career which, in the prophetic language of the letter to which he owed his election, was to " change the face of education all through the public schools of England." *

It was a momentous decision, and one that must have required all the encouragement that so keen-

* The words are those used by Dr. Hawkins, late Provost of Oriel, who has passed away while these pages were passing through the press.

sighted a friend as the elder Augustus Hare, who was
about to marry Mrs. Stanley's sister and who was
taken into counsel, could venture to give. English
public schools in those days were but rough homes for
sensitive boys. At all times there is much in their life
especially trying to boys of exceptional genius; to all
in fact who are out of sympathy — out of touch, so to
speak — with the average tendencies and tastes of
boyhood. Rugby was, if a staunch Rugbeian may be
allowed to say so, of small repute outside the circle
of a few Midland counties till the advent of Arnold.
The innumerable readers of "Tom Brown" will find
in it a faithful picture of the rougher side of school
life as it presented itself in the earlier days of our
great Head Master. Arthur Stanley joined the school
from which he was to receive, and to which he was to
give, so much, in January, 1829. Whatever his sufferings in that new life, he yet with the courage that
lay behind a timid exterior, put a brave face on the
matter. In letters to his former schoolmaster, towards
whom he cherished a loyal affection, the new boy describes himself as domiciled for the time at a small
boarding-house of fourteen boys — the larger house, of
which he was soon to be a more permanent inmate, being not yet completed — each of the fourteen having a
small study to himself, "which," he says, "is a very
great advantage." He goes on to give a characteristic
sketch of those now world-famous school buildings:
the "towers and turrets," looking, to his boyish fancy,
"like those of some stately castle;" "the Close, with

its many tall trees " — on his return, years after, from
Greece, he rejoiced once more over those ancient elms
— "and its small chapel," — where a monument to
himself will soon be added to that of Arnold, — of the
surrounding country, where his eye already marked
in those sluggish brooks "the numerous branches of
the Avon " — the Avon of Wycliffe and of Shakespeare — " winding through extensive meadows." He
appears to wish to amuse his former instructor, he
certainly astounds his later friends, by announcing
that "he has been chosen to write out one of the Præpostor's prize-essays, *on account of writing such a good
hand* " — carefully underlining the now almost incredible statement. He tells him " how the school now
numbers 167 boys, but is rapidly increasing with Dr.
Arnold's fame ; " he drops, poor boy ! the remark "that
he has not yet fixed on anyone whom he should like
as a friend." Doubtless, for a time, he suffered
acutely from something worse than isolation and
want of sympathy. But those who have had boys at
school will understand his silence on the subject.
Years later, when all such trials were over, on the eve
of competing for the Balliol scholarship, he wrote to
a friend already at Oxford, " I recollect when I first
came here, and was much bullied at my first house,
that I one day walked disconsolately up to the
school, where I met ——, who took me round the
Close, and asked me how I liked the place ? I, being
too broken-spirited to enter into a detail of my griev-
ances, said, in the very bitterness of my heart, that

I liked it very much." How many disconsolate schoolboys have made the same answer! But those days soon ended. He rose rapidly in the school, thanks, he tells his old friend, to his careful teaching; how could it have been otherwise? He attained, if not robustness of constitution, yet an entire immunity from conscious ill-health ; "my health," he tells his former teacher, "is almost perfect. From one half-year to another I pass with scarcely a day's sickness." He was able once more to indulge in comparative freedom his taste for reading, "keen as a hound" — I borrow his own words, which I have already quoted — "keen as a hound in the pursuit of knowledge." He writes of himself as "reading to myself, chiefly history. I have got through all Mitford and all Gibbon, and several smaller ones, with greater success than I could have expected." "I don't know," he says, still writing to his old schoolmaster, "whether you have heard much of Dr. Arnold, or conceived bad opinions of him. It is possible that you may have heard him abused in every way. He has been branded with the names of Sabbath-breaker and Infidel. But seeing so much of him as I do, I may safely say that he is as thorough a Christian as you can anywhere find. His sermons are certainly the most beautiful that I ever heard, and rendered doubly impressive by his delivery. He has reformed the school in every possible way, introducing History, Mathematics, Modern Languages, Examinations, Prizes, &c." My younger hearers will be startled at hearing that such now established

branches of a school curriculum were then looked on
as revolutionary innovations. "I am afraid," he adds,
"that you would not find many in the school to give
him as good a character as this, as perhaps he has got
a little more than the usual odium attached to a Head
Master, but I think there are few who would question his talents or his sermons. *I* am, as you may
perceive, thoroughly prejudiced in his favour. The
common report is that he will be a Bishop. I hope it
will not be before my departure." It is fair to add
that, in a conversation held years after with an Oxford undergraduate, he confessed that, though at first
charmed with his Head Master, there was yet a time
in his schoolboy life in which he looked on him as
"fierce and alarming": and thought that what he used
to hear of him at home was somewhat exaggerated,
and that there was some truth in what the boys used to
say about his harshness. "It was after my getting into
the fifth form, and during my three and a-half years
under him in the sixth, that I began to feel what
Arnold really was. During all the time that he was
being publicly abused, and while nobody befriended
him, I was perfectly satisfied in my own mind that I
was in intercourse with one of the most remarkable
men of the age. What anxiety there was among some
of us to hear him preach! When Sunday came round
— when he went from his seat up to the pulpit, and
we saw that he was going to preach — I and Vaughan
used to nudge each other with delight. When I came
back from the examination at Balliol, we posted home
late at night, in order to avoid missing his sermon."

Rugby, in fact, soon became to him, as to how many others since, when the first troubles of his early days were at an end, I will not say a second home, but a place invested with a dearness and a sacredness of its own, not inferior to, though different from, that which attached to such homes as the Rectory at Alderley. School distinctions, of course, fell to his lot one after another. He records in one of his letters how, by winning the prizes for a Greek poem and a Latin essay, he had succeeded at last in carrying off the five great school distinctions then existing—a feat in which he was only rivalled once in the history of Arnoldian Rugby, by A. H. Clough, whose name, dear to all Rugby men, I have already mentioned. Indeed, the most definite school tradition that I, as a schoolboy there myself, found attached to his name was, that on handing to him the very last of these five prizes, his master and ours broke for the first time the profound, the almost grim silence which, strange as it may sound to modern ears, he invariably maintained on the annual "Speech-Day," to utter the expressive words, "Thank you, Stanley; we have nothing more to give you."

Meantime his literary instincts were finding their full satisfaction, not only in the work done at the feet of his renowned master, but in his own insatiable reading, as partly described above. Now, too, it was that he developed the first germs of that marvellous capacity for forming warm and lasting friendships which was to the very end of his life one of his most marked characteristics. It is touching even now to read how

the boy, so shy and reserved in his beloved home, so
forlorn and solitary in his first year or two of Rugby
life, whose incapacity for entering into intimacy with
other boys had once so gravely alarmed a mother's
heart, was already realising her hopes that the cloud
that isolated him was only transient. A letter exists,
written at the close of his schooldays to an older friend,*
then an undergraduate, in which, after speaking of his
soon leaving Rugby, " the place where I have spent five
happy years, learned knowledge human and divine, as
probably I shall never learn it again," he speaks also of
Rugby as "the place, too, of my several friendships
(forgive me," he inserts, " for the word *several*) to last,
I hope, none lessened by the existence of others, to the
latest hour of my life." How many there are still
living, how many who have passed away, whom the
young writer of these words was to inspire with feelings
which even the sacred word friendship seems only
inadequately to express! What a genius for friendship,
in the very highest and noblest conception of its mean-
ing, was he to develope! How he loved his friends, how
steadfastly did he stand by them; to how many did he
open his heart and how many hearts did he win — win
and raise and ennoble—by his friendship, without stir-
ring the slightest sense of jealousy or rivalry in the men
of all ages and of all classes who delighted in the sense
of each other's affection for him! How they, how we,
rejoiced to bring our friends into the charmed circle

* Dr. Greenhill, who has kindly allowed me to read many of
these early letters.

of his companionship and love. How prophetic, seen now, to those who saw the circle of his friends recruited year after year, the youthful words, "my several friendships, to last, I hope, none lessened by the existence of the others, to the latest hour of my life!"

On the other hand, it is not to be supposed that, happy and cheerful as he was at school, he ever became a genuine specimen of what is now ordinarily understood by a "public-school boy." He ranged freely over the country, not very interesting in itself, round Rugby; but he never acquired any taste for the ordinary games and amusements which now-a-days fill the foreground in the popular conception of young Rugby life. Indeed the taste for such games, far less organised than they are now, was less widely diffused than it has since become, and the distinction between the many who played or idled, and the few who worked, greatly effaced since, was in the earlier and rougher period of Arnold's time still strongly marked. There is a short paper in the old "Rugby Magazine," which it was not till the last time I saw him, within less than four weeks of his death, that, while talking of this very subject, I learned to be his. He speaks there of himself and his young co-editors as turning out with heated brains for a ten minutes' walk in the Close before "locking up," and meeting the other, the more numerous and athletic, portion of the school coming in from their summer afternoon spent in cricket. It is a paper which could scarcely have been written at the present day: the state of things which it describes—the division of the School into two classes—is one which, for good or evil, for good and evil, mainly I trust for good, has passed away. Once at a Rugby dinner he described, with the humour of which he was a master, how, "as I sat in that study reading Mitford, a stone thrown at me by a schoolfellow came through the window, struck me on the forehead here," striking his forehead as he spoke, " and left an almost indelible scar." The story is characteristic of the involuntary disgust with which the sight of a schoolfellow sitting at home to read, otherwise than under compulsion, would have inspired nine out of ten of the schoolboys of the day. And the result of this state of things was that his direct influence on the School was probably confined to the circle of those who were more or less like-minded. " The young barbarians all at play " cared little, though they learned to look on him with a certain awe, for their gifted schoolfellow, the quiet, kindly, studious, high-bred Præpostor. " Not being marked out from others in any game," writes one who, as a very young boy, was with him in the same house, and rose years after to the headship of the School — "not even to the extent of Clough's prowess as goal keeper at football, his name passed away very quickly at his house, save for the holidays which he won for us at Oxford." Such was, I doubt not, the case with these outer barbarians. But I am bound to say, in defence of my old school, that coming to it as I did at an unusually late age, and being admitted at once to the society of my older schoolfellows, I found his name, after the lapse of three years from his leaving Rugby, surrounded by the halo of departed genius; and I may add that I for one could say by heart most of his Oxford prize poem before I had ever seen its author.

Do I fatigue you with these boyish reminiscences? Let me add one. In a letter written towards the end of his time at Rugby he speaks of rumours coming from Oxford of the rising reputation of "William Gladstone," who had been a pupil for a time of Stanley's first teacher. In later life he recounted the story of his first meeting the present Prime Minister and member for Mid-Lothian — then a boy of fifteen, himself a few years younger — at the house of Mr. Gladstone's father. "Have you ever read Gray's poems?" said the future statesman. "No," replied his younger acquaintance. "Then do so at once," said the elder vehemently, and produced the volume. It was taken home, read at once, and enjoyed; and to the end of his life it was difficult for him to speak of the scenery of Greece, or to go round the tombs of the earlier kings in the Abbey, without the appropriate quotation from Gray rising to his lips. For myself, I shall always think of the poet as associated not least of all with the veteran statesman and the friend whom he will, I trust, long survive.

The end of his schoolboy days drew near. You will find a graphic account in Mr. Hare's paper of the eventful week in which he won, the first of many Rugby boys who have followed in his steps, the first of the two vacant scholarships at Balliol. The tumult of joy which such marked success raised in his own

heart, in the large circle of Rugby men at Oxford,
at Rugby, and not least at Alderley, is more easy
perhaps for Rugbeians and Oxonians to realise than
for those to whom the details of Oxford competitions
are a matter, if not of absolute yet of comparative
indifference. " It is a great triumph," he says, in a
letter to that old schoolmaster to whom in that hour
of triumph he was still loyal, "a great triumph to us,
for Rugby has hitherto been kept rather in the background by other schools, who this year were entirely
defeated." In the same letter he once more, with
characteristic chivalry, returns to the charge in behalf of Dr. Arnold. But I will not repeat to you the
emphatic words in which he asserts his unaltered
adherence to his former opinion.

In the following June he left Rugby. There is a
humorous and graphic account in one of his letters
of the final school examination, conducted on behalf
of Oxford by the present Bishop of Salisbury, then
tutor of Balliol, and soon to become Head Master of
Winchester, and on behalf of Cambridge by Dr.
Wordsworth, now well known as the venerable Bishop
of Lincoln. After recounting how his own name was
proclaimed first in the anxiously expected list, and
immediately explaining that this was merely because
he was senior in the school, and that Vaughan, his dear
friend and future brother-in-law, was really bracketed
as his equal, he expresses the hope that his friend
" will not think it affected in him to say that he could
not possibly have wished it better." " There is all,"

he writes, "that was necessary to gratify every individual feeling of vanity; all to make me happy for Vaughan, to whom I should not at all have grudged the first place; all to make me happy for the School." "For now," he adds, with a dash of public spirit which every public-school boy or man will appreciate, "let no one say of me, whether in my successes or my failures at Oxford, that I was the first at Rugby, and therefore must be taken as a specimen for better or worse of the School. The answer is ready in black and white — that there was and is another equal, who would, had it not been for his long illness before the examination, have most probably been before me."

I may venture to say that there is no true son of Rugby living who does not rejoice in a "bracket" which linked together those two friends, a due estimate of whose widely different gifts must have sorely puzzled the most discriminating of examiners.

The hour came at which he bade goodby to his school life. I have been allowed to read a letter in which he describes the scene in which one who has been called the hero-schoolmaster had to part with one who has been felicitously called the hero-pupil.* "I saw him," he writes, "but for a few minutes, but those few minutes were worth much;" and after describing their brief conversation, the promises of introduction to his old pupil, the late Bishop of Salisbury, and to a newer friend, the present Lord Chancellor of Eng-

---

* In the touching sermon preached in the Abbey by the Dean of Llandaff on the Sunday after the death of his brother-in-law.

land, and then the parting words, the very tones of the
twice repeated " God bless you, Stanley ; " he goes on,
" and so we parted, and so that constant and delightful and blessed intercourse I have had with him for
three years closed for ever. My comfort is that I shall
see him now, when I do see him, with greater ease ;
but even that may and must be soon broken off, by
his becoming, what every year makes more inevitable,
a Bishop. I see I have said for ever. God grant not
for ever literally, though it may be so on earth."

There is something, you will say, overstrained in all
this. He himself so far agreed with you that he spoke
at the end of his life of a certain exaggeration of tone
in his youthful letters, not on this subject specially,
but on all. Yet which of us would wish to rob youth
of its special gift of a generous enthusiasm ? Who
of us would not rejoice to see our sons fired with a
like ardour for another Arnold ?

Before many weeks were over he had the delight of
visiting his beloved master in his home among the
Westmoreland lakes — not where some of his later pupils of the same age were privileged to see him, at Fox
How, which was then in the builder's hands — but at
Allan Bank, overlooking Grasmere, which had been
the temporary home of the poet Wordsworth. Space
and time warn me to leave to his biographer his short
but delightful notices of Arnold in his home ; of Wordsworth, to seeing whom he had looked forward with all
the interest of a schoolboy admirer ; of Hartley Cole-
ridge ; of Captain Hamilton, author of " Cyril Thorn-

ton," and "Men and Mannersin America," "still lame,"
says the youthful student of Napier's History, " from a
wound received at Albuera ;" or his humorous account
of the expedition to Keswick, and the vain watching like
a cat outside Greta Bank in hopes of seing Southey, of
one who to the end of his days upheld against all
comers the poetic merits of " Thalaba " and " Kehama."

The visit was paid in 1834.   Less than eight years
later, on the 12th of June, 1842, the master to whom
he still looked with a no less ardent if less boyish
devotion was taken from the work which he was carrying on with unclouded success at Rugby.   Arnold
was still comparatively a young man—he wanted three
years of fifty ; to all appearance unusually strong and
vigorous, growing every year in intellectual grasp, and
dying at the very moment when the combination of that
Christian faith which sustained him in the swift and
painful passage from life to death with an ardent and
inextinguishable love of truth, might have opened for
him a fresh field of untold influence in the religious
life of England.   He had outlived much of the odium
with which his position as a religious teacher, a church
reformer, and an outspoken opponent of the rising
Oxford movement had at one time covered him.   His
Oxford pupils still recall the rapid revulsion from
fierce aversion to warm admiration produced at the
University by the delivery of his historical lectures
in the spring of that fatal year.   The shock that ran
through England at the news of his death few here
may remember.   It remains in the memory of his pupils

as something almost or quite unparalleled. "To me," said Stanley, who had hurried to Rugby on receiving the dreadful news in London from the present Dean of Durham, "to me," he said, in the first letter that one who was then his pupil and is now his successor ever received from him, "it seems as though the solid earth had passed away beneath my feet." He preached the funeral sermon at that saddest of gatherings in Rugby Chapel; stood by the grave side by side with his father and his friends, and immediately volunteered to write his Biography; "a work," he said, "which from first to last I thoroughly enjoyed." And well he might! When was such a tribute paid in English literature by a pupil to his teacher? Let me add that no 12th of June ever passed without his writing to Mrs. Arnold, or, when she had passed away, to her daughter at Fox How; few on which one or other of his own Rugby pupils failed to write to himself.

Two questions at once arise. How far is Arnold's reputation due to his biographer, rather than to his own merits? And what was the effect of Arnold's influence on Stanley? The first is a question of fact, the other one of inference and conjecture. Some of us have heard it said, in answer to the former question, not merely that Arnold's work and character were brought home to thousands, to whom otherwise they would have remained unknown, by that matchless Biography, but that the man himself was transfigured by the genius and devotion of the biographer — that the portrait is, in fact, an ideal picture. Nay, it has been more than whispered in these latter days, that the Arnold of the biographer is a legendary being, a mythical personage, created by the picturesque, but unfaithful, fancy of Arthur Stanley.

It is encouraging to feel how baseless sometimes are the final results of an over-restless scepticism even in the hands of those who would have no words too strong for their condemnation of a "negative criticism" on the part of others. We, his pupils, are fast passing away. Let one of those who still remain record his emphatic protest against these extravagances of incredulity, this entire misreading of the character of two such men. It is impossible, alas! that the biography of Stanley can be written by one so gifted and furnished for the task as he was for his; but it will be much if it be written by one equally unsparing of pains to verify every touch and every line, as determined to check every impression of his own mind by careful comparison with that made on others; above all, content to let the subject of his work speak for himself, in his own words, and almost in his own tones, as Arnold speaks in his letters and journals, and to keep his own impressions, his own views, as carefully in the background as Stanley keeps his in that memorable Biography.

But what was the effect of Arnold on himself? Did the influence of so commanding and overpowering a character dwarf his own genius, de-individualise — if I may coin the word — the individual Stanley, or unduly affect and modify his course and character?

Should we, but for Arnold, have had something other, something perhaps better, something perhaps worse, but something different to what we had in Stanley ?

Similar questions may occur as to all lives. Like analogous questions in the history of nations, they are always hard to answer. The influence, no doubt, of his teacher was enormous over his mind in youth. He was quite conscious of it then and afterwards. " Arnold at Rugby," he said, late in life, "was my idol and oracle, both in one. Afterwards, well — he was not exactly my oracle, but I reverenced him wholly to the end — I have never felt such reverence for any one since." In that most moving of sermons, preached near Stanley's open grave, the Vaughan of whom he spoke with such chivalrous affection nearly fifty years before, recalled his friend's rapt countenance as he listened to his master's sermons — his entire absorption, as he went straight from the chapel to his study to transcribe his impressions of those memorable discourses. Speaking at Baltimore in 1878, "the lapse of years," he said, "has only served to deepen in me the conviction that no gift can be more valuable than the recollection and the inspiration of a great character working on our own. I hope that you may all experience this at some time of your life as I have done." And he was quite alive to it while it was in full force. " What a wonderful influence," he says, in a letter written while still at Rugby, "that man has over me ! I certainly feel that I have hardly a free will of my own on any subject on which he has written or spoken.

It is, I suppose," he goes on to say, "a weak and un-
natural state to be in ; for," he adds, with instinctive
insight, "I do not at all consider myself to be naturally
of the same frame as he is;" and, curiously enough, a
great part of a long letter to the same correspondent
is filled with a remarkably bold and searching criticism
of a striking hymn, written by his great teacher, of
which he had obtained possession. Indeed, no two
men could have been in many points more unlike
each other. In stature, in manners, in appearance,
in voice, in conversational powers, in much of their
general tone of mind, the difference between them
amounted almost to contrast ; and however strong
were the bonds of sympathy and agreement on the
most important subjects, however undying the effects
of that contact with so vigorous and impressive a
teacher in the most impressible stage of the pupil's
life, yet those who knew them both are not very careful
to answer otherwise than with a smile of incredulity
the suggestion that Stanley was in any way the creation of his teacher. What difference might have been
made by the subtraction, so to speak, of the Arnoldian
element from the Stanley whom they knew, they cannot say. But they feel quite sure that he had a genius
all his own, and an individuality, and an independence
and a power of marking out his own course, not inferior to that of his master. And considering his early
training and home influences, and still more the whole
temperament and constitution of his mind, they will
greatly question whether, after whatever periods of

temporary oscillation, the ultimate bent and direction of the forces which marked his genius and character, would have been very different to what they were, even had his father shrunk from entrusting him to the then untried world of that Warwickshire Grammar School, and placed him in the more familiar atmosphere of "Commoners" at Winchester.

In all this I am puprosely anticipating. Let me now return to the narrative of his life.

In 1834 he was fairly launched on his undergraduate career. It was an eventful time at Oxford. The dominant religious influences of the place were becoming every year more antagonistic to those under which his boyhood had been passed. The watchwords of "Church Authority," "Apostolical Succession," "The Primitive Church," "Sacramental Grace," were to be heard on all sides. The views which they represented were being urged in sermons, in tracts, in conversation, above all from the pulpit, by the most persuasive of lips and the purest of lives. Their effect on the life of Oxford has been described, in a manner which I shall not attempt to emulate, by Principal Shairp,* himself somewhat later a member of the same College as Arthur Stanley. Their influence on the religious history of the nation has yet to be fully estimated. How far the theological atmosphere in which he now lived temporarily affected him, one who was a schoolboy at the time will hardly venture to say; but among his most intimate friends were more than

* In a paper on Keble in "Studies on Poetry and Philosophy."

one of those who afterwards became the leaders of a
movement in which he certainly never joined; and
there is no doubt that, while still an undergraduate,
he felt the keenest interest in the defence of Dr.,
afterwards Bishop, Hampden, whose appointment to
the Regius chair of Theology provoked a storm, the
first of a long series that later on convulsed the English
Church. He was actually, there is reason to believe,
privately consulted by Lord Melbourne himself, whose
short but characteristic encomium on his young adviser
need not be repeated. Doubtless even his active mind
and indomitable power of work were largely absorbed
by his necessary reading. In a letter to his eldest
brother, written while reading at Oxford during his
last summer vacation, he speaks of " looking forward
to November to free me at once and for ever from
the great burden which has been hanging over me for
the last three years." He was by no means what is
called a heaven-born scholar, in the technical sense of
the word. In Greek and Latin composition he had
been always easily distanced at Rugby by his friend
Vaughan, and for the more abstract branches of mental
philosophy, so congenial to the Scottish mind, he had
no special turn. He used to amuse his Oxford pupils
by recounting his laborious efforts to attain sufficient
excellence in Latin verse-writing, in which he never
greatly excelled, to allow him to obtain, as he did
at last by the excellence of other work, the Ireland
Scholarship — the highest distinction offered by the
University for Greek and Latin scholarship; and he

would enlarge on the debt which he owed to the present Bishop of St. Albans, who, as his private tutor, assisted him greatly to overcome this special deficiency.

The most interesting achievement of his undergraduate days was a poem for which in 1837 he won the Newdigate prize. Its subject was " The Gipsies," and it seems to me to be separated by a marked and distinct line from all his earlier literary efforts (setting aside passages in private letter or journals) which I have yet seen, and to bear the true stamp of the mature Stanley, such as his later friends and the world at large have known him. It is not only that it is something far more than an unusually meritorious prize poem, and contains touches of description drawn from natural scenery, such as a trne poet would gladly claim to have written at his age. Snch lines, for instance, as —

> " The changeful smiles, the living face of light,
> The steady gaze of the still solemn night;
> Bright lakes, the glistening eyes of solitude,
> Girt with grey cliffs and folds of mighty wood,"

though possibly within the reach of one who, without high poetic gifts, had saturated himself with the works of first-class poets, are something more than the patchwork phrases of a skilled versifier. Nor is it only that when, with a reference in a footnote to Lamartine's pilgrimage to the Holy Land, he speaks of —

> " The meteor light
> Of Syrian skies by Zion's towery height,"

he foreshadows his own more fruitful visits to that

CHAP. I.] *ARTHUR PENRHYN STANLEY.* 43

sacred soil. But when those who are familiar with his later writings read his description of the —

> " Dark and troublous time —
> The Heaven all gloom, the wearied Earth all crime,"

that ushered in the fifteenth century ; or the couplets that follow, beginning with —

> " A stranger people, 'mid that murky gloom,
> Knocked at the gates of awe-struck Christendom;"

we feel-that "the boy" has already become "father of the man." So again, after breathing the very spirit of romance and poetry into the various legends that hung round the origin of that strange people, as for instance, in the words —

> " Heard ye the nations heave their long last groans
> Amidst the crash of Asia's thousand thrones,"

he lingers over the tradition, destitute as it is of all historical value, of their representing the old Egyptian race, and thus living as degraded wanderers by the side of their ancient Hebrew bondservants, in such lines as —

> " Remnant of ages, from thy glory cast,
> Dread link between the present and the past —
>   *   *   *   *   *
> One only race amid thy dread compeers
> Still moves with thee along this vale of tears;
> Long since ye parted by the Red Sea's strand,
> Now face to face ye meet in every land.
> Alone amid a new-born world ye dwell —
> Egypt's lorn people, outcast Israel!"

As we read such passages, we feel that we are at once transported into the very centre of the familiar thoughts and imagery of the Stanley that was to be: that if the voice is the voice of the young undergraduate, still toiling for his degree, the words and the ideas are those of the writer who was one day almost to re-create large fields of sacred and ecclesiastical history by clothing them with a fresh glow of life and colour.

It is interesting to add that the poem as it stands bears traces, as we know from the writer, of corrections introduced by the author of the " Christian Year," who then held the Professorship of Poetry; it contains also a reference, perhaps the earliest that appeared in print, to a line from an early poem of the present Poet Laureate, whose name, however, was not given, and which the poet Keble supposed to be a quotation from Shakespeare.

His career as an undergraduate of Balliol was now at an end; his First Class obtained, his degree taken. The burden was lifted from his shoulders, and with character consolidated, and many warm and lasting friendships formed, he stood on the threshold of mature manhood.

A Fellowship at his own College would have seemed the natural sequel in the academical life of one of the most distinguished of her sons; one whose character was as spotless as his career had been exceptionally brilliant. But it will hardly be believed in Edinburgh, it will scarcely be credited in modern Oxford, that so strong was the feeling among the older and ruling members of that society against admitting to their circle the son of such a Bishop as Bishop Stanley, and the sympathizing pupil of Thomas Arnold, that he was

privately given to understand that his chance of election at his own College was too small to warrant him in
exposing himself to a repulse. The moment was seized
by the keen-sighted dexterity of one still living, then
an active and influential tutor of University College —
let me once more thank him here! — and in the year
1839 Arthur Stanley was elected Fellow of that College ; an event I do not hesitate to say of far greater
importance to the welfare of that ancient society,
which claims King Alfred for its founder, than any
that had befallen it for at least a century. In the same
year his dear and life-long Balliol friend, Benjamin
Jowett, now the Master of Balliol, was elected, while
still an undergraduate, to a Fellowship in his own College ; and before it closed, Arthur Stanley had, after a
period of some perplexity and hesitation, taken a step
to which he had steadily looked forward from his Rugby days, and which he never for a moment regretted,
and had been ordained deacon by the Bishop of Oxford.

He had now fully resolved to give his life, for the
present at least, to the work of a College Tutor at Oxford. But before plunging into educational work, he
resided for a time as junior Fellow, occupying himself
in study, in learning the elements of Hebrew, attending with great interest Dr. Pusey's lectures, and in
writing an Essay, which obtained the Chancellor's
Prize, on a congenial historical subject. It is a composition which almost deserves to be placed beside his
prize poem. Would that time allowed me to quote to
you the eloquent and most characteristic page with

which it closes. Meantime, important changes had taken place in his family circle. His father and family had removed to Norwich, and were established in their new home in the Bishop's Palace. His sailor-brother Owen had accompanied Captain Back as scientific officer on his adventurous voyage in the *Terror* to the Arctic seas, and struggling back with a scurvy-stricken crew, in a battered ship only kept from going to pieces by under-girding her with iron chains, had reached at last the wild but friendly shores of Lough Swilly on the night of the 3rd of September, 1837. There, for the first time, the young officer heard to his great dismay that the Alderley home was broken up. The removal had already taken place. While it was in contemplation Arthur Stanley, still an undergraduate, had stolen two days in term time to visit his father in London. "It was," he writes, "a most trying time. I should hardly have known my father's face, so worn as he was with the anxiety of the week before in making up his mind to the decision." "But," he writes, after a visit paid in September to Norwich, "I do not repent of it now; he seems much freer and happier than he ever did before." In the same letter, addressed to his brother on board H.M.S. *Terror*, he gives a characteristic account of their new home, contrasting the ugliness of the Palace with the surpassing beauty of the Cathedral that overshadows it. "The former is," says the yet untravelled traveller, "among houses what Moscow is, I should think, among cities. Rooms which one may really call very fine side by side with the

meanest of passages and staircases. By the riverside,"
he characteristically writes, "is a ruin where a Bishop
once killed a wolf; over the river, a road down which
another Bishop marched with 6000 men at arms;"
and he assures his brother that he is highly flattered
by his having carried the remembrance of the Hampden controversy with him through the Arctic winter.
" That storm," he says, " is laid ; in fact, its place is
taken in the newspapers by the installation sermon
of the Bishop of Norwich." The letter is dated September 22, 1837, and concludes with a fear that "these
full particulars of Norwich life may give you the idea,
which they say at home is the case, that I am the
only one puffed up by the accession of dignity."

May I be allowed to insert here what is to myself
something more than a slight personal reminiscence?
It was after his migration from Balliol, that it became
the duty of the new Fellow of University, early in the
year 1840, to take part in the annual Scholarship
Examination, which ended in the election of a Rugby
schoolboy, the first of many whom his rising fame drew
not from Rugby only, to a College which had so wisely
added to its teaching staff so attractive and magnetic an
influence. More than two-and-forty years have passed
since on that bright March afternoon the loud con-
gratulations of old friends and schoolfellows were
hushed for a moment as the young Examiner stepped
into the quadrangle and turned to greet the new
scholar. How well does he recall that kindly greet-
ing—the hearty grasp of the friendly hand that seemed

to carry the heart in it — the bright expressive countenance of the young tutor, so full of all that might
win and charm a somewhat imaginative schoolboy,
which shines still out of the distance in all its first
youthful beauty "as the face of an angel." He at
once invited the newly elected scholar to take a walk
with him on his return from a formal visit to the
Master of the College, and that dull road that led out
by the then unplanted, unreclaimed, Oxford Parks, is
still lit in the memory of him who trod it by his side,
with something fairer than the bright March sun
which shone across it. "We are walking," he said,
"towards Rugby," and at once placed his companion
at his ease by questions about his friends there, and
about the Master who was the object of as enthusiastic a devotion to the younger as to the older Rugbeian. How little did it occur to either, as they
parted, how strangely near their lives were to be drawn
to each other! The younger might have listened to
a soothsayer who had said, "You have won to-day
something that you will soon count far more precious
than the scholarship in which you are exulting:" but
how contemptuously would he have turned from the
prediction that he would years after be called from
the headship of the College of which he was that
day enrolled as the youngest member, to succeed, in
his new friend, not the least illustrious and the most
lamented of the Deans of Westminster. It is in
virtue of the friendship of which that day was the
birthday that I have stood before you this evening.

CHAPTER II.

(From 1840 to 1863.)

OXFORD — CANTERBURY — OXFORD.

IN the autumn of the same year Arthur Stanley left England for a tour in Greece and Italy. The tour was so far memorable that it encouraged and confirmed the taste for foreign travel, implanted first of all by that early visit to the South of France, which he never lost. He suffered, as travellers at that time were sure to suffer, from occasional personal discomforts. " At Athens," he said in later life, " I felt the cold of winter more than I ever did ; at St. Petersburg least of all." But he had already mastered the art of extracting a fund of amusement from such passing trials, and his companion, the present Dean of Norwich, was a man of most kindly heart and unfailing humour. In spite therefore of all drawbacks, he drank deep of the delights of moving about from day to day among the scenes of Greek history and poetry, and he became conscious in himself and revealed more fully to his friends a power of bringing before the minds of others such pictures of scenes which most

interested him as, when their number and their variety
are taken into account, have rarely, if ever, been surpassed in English literature. A long letter which he
wrote to Dr. Arnold, in which he dwells on some of
the main characteristics of Greek scenery, deserves to
be placed side by side with the most striking of the
descriptive passages in his later writings.

It is possible that a few words on that which forms
so marked an element in all his writings, his attitude
as regards natural scenery, may be of interest here
as a contribution to a right estimate alike of his
literary position and of the pervading tone and colour of his mind.

Scenery in and for itself, the aspects of Nature as
viewed in their own light and for their own sakes, he
never, I think I am right in saying, never once attempts to describe. In one of his letters to an old
pupil, written at Canterbury in 1854, there is a passage which gives the key alike to the excellences and
the deficiencies of this great painter of Nature. "I cannot think," he says, "that mere effusions of emotion
at the transient blushes of Nature deserve an everlasting record. I feel about such effusions, almost as
I feel about my present, oftentimes ineffectual, labours at reproducing scenes of my travels" (he was
then at work at " Sinai and Palestine "), "that they
are not worth publishing, *except as a framework to
events or ideas* of greater magnitude." Of Nature, as
studied for her own sake, in the spirit of Wordsworth,
or so many true poets in all ages, or of Mr. Ruskin

among modern prose writers, there will be found, I
venture to say, no trace in his published writings or in
his letters since he grew to manhood. Whenever he
becomes enthusiastic on the beauties of nature, we may
feel sure that there is always at work a motive other
than that of the artist — that behind nature lies some
human or historical interest. " How mysterious," he
says, in a letter to a younger friend, then at Rome,
"the Alban lake! How beautiful Nemi! how romantic Subiaco! how solemn Ostia! how desolate Gabii!"
What could be better? you will say. Yes; but behind
all these, there lay on his mental retina the background
of the history of Rome — "the one only place," he goes
on to say, "in the whole world, that is absolutely inexhaustible!" It is quite true that occasionally, in
some three, or four, or five remarkable passages, oc-
curring especially, and for an obvious reason, in his
American addresses, he introduces pictures of some
natural phenomena, quite apart from any direct historical association. Such is the splendid picture of the
Falls of Niagara; the graceful and touching image, a
true sonnet in prose, drawn from two trees, the graceful maple and the gnarled and twisted oak, growing
side by side; the description of the course of the St.
Lawrence as contrasted with that of the Nile; of sun-
rise, as seen from the summit of the Righi. But in each
of these apparent exceptions to his ordinary habit, he
seizes on some aspect of external nature, not for its own
sake, but as the symbol of some idea — some truth,
that he wishes to enforce or interpret. As a general

rule, he looks on nature not as a poetical interpreter
of nature — not, we may fairly say, as a poet in the
truest sense — but as one who seems never to feel that
he has thoroughly mastered any event, or chain of
events, in human or sacred history, till he has seen the
spot, and breathed the air which gives to each occur-
rence its peculiar and local colouring.   And with what
an eye he sees it ! with what a power of insight and
discrimination he reproduces the exact points in which
nature and history meet and blend with, and mutually
influence, each other!   " We go," he said in his Sermons in the East, "to the Jerusalem where Christ died
and rose again.   To see that Holy City, even though
the exact spots of His death and resurrection are unknown, *is to give a new force to the sound of the Name,*
whenever afterwards we hear it in Church, or read it
in the Bible."   The words apply in their first sense to
the most sacred of all lands, and of all scenes.   But the
feeling that dictated them is the key to something else,
to the unwearied, the insatiable avidity — I can call
it nothing less — with which he would fatigue the most
indefatigable of fellow travellers or hosts, by visiting
any and every spot, however apparently insignificant,
which was connected, directly or indirectly, with any
historical event or person, or with any scene in the
works of the great masters of poetry or fiction, or even
with any important legend that had ever influenced the
human mind.   " At Lindisfarne," says one who visited it with him, "his mind was, I am sure, quite as
much occupied with the immurement of Constance,

as with the memory of St. Aidan and St. Cuthbert."
Tours was to him quite as much associated with
Quentin Durward as with St. Martin, or with Hilde-
garde, or Lonis XI., or Henry II. His persistence in
dragging a fellow traveller to call on the Archbishop
of Granada was based quite as much on his being the
lineal successor of the master of Gil Blas, as on his
being the occupant of that historic see. And the keen
eye for detecting resemblances and points of agreement
under superficial or real differences, that gave such a
character to his whole treatment of history and of
theology, followed him also in his visits to historic
places. As he saw an analogy to the yet unvisited
Moscow in his new home in Norwich, so he delighted
to point out the seven hills of Rome in the same city.
He was not content with recognising in this your
famous capital the resemblance — the modified resemblance, which I have already quoted — to Athens;
he found in the relation of the new to the old town
something which reminded him of a place so unlike
Edinburgh as Prague.

Let me add that in the same spirit in which before
his tour to the Holy Land he read through and
through all that he could find worth reading on Palestine, so he would visit no place, not even in the
suburbs of London, or a railway junction in Scotland,
without learning all that he could of its history or
associations. A curious feature of his travelling
mind — if I may so speak — was that for many years
of his life he did not care, indeed rather objected, to

see the same scene twice. " When once," he said,
" I have seen a remarkable sight, I do not care to see
it again, unless it is one with which fond or happy
associations are connected." " The second sight of
Prague quite revolted me," he added, with comic
energy ; "and though I saw Marathon on a rainy
day, yet I refused three or four opportunities of seeing it again. On the first sight of scenes of this sort
a whole new world opens before me ; floods of thought
come in, which are indelible, and there is nothing new
in a second visit."

And now let me return to his personal history. At
the conclusion of his tour in Greece, he wrote the letter to Dr. Arnold to which I have already referred,
in solitude, or worse than solitude. His fellow suf-
ferers under the miseries of a Maltese quarantine, were
some young men, whose loose talk revolted him, and
who had not the good sense to discover that beneath
the mask of that averted countenance and those silent
lips, was one, to enjoy whose society and conversation
many wiser than themselves would have gladly faced
the horrors of that tedious imprisonment. Released
at last, he arrived alone at Naples, depressed, home-
sick, and yearning for some congenial society. In the
Museum he met an English acquaintance, who said,
" Of course you have seen Hugh Pearson?" mention-
ing the name of one of his closest Balliol friends.
" Hugh Pearson !" he exclaimed; " where is he ? "
and darted in search of him. He found him in front
of a well-known statue, rushed up to him, and, over-

come with joy and emotion, fell into his friend's arms with a burst of uncontrollable tears. I mention the incident, not merely as illustrative of his tender and affectionate nature, which never lost a spark of its youthful warmth till the hand relaxed its clasp, and the heart had ceased to beat, but because the companion whom he then found, and with whom he completed his homeward journey, became from that time the very closest and most inseparable of all his friends.

When sorrowing mourners gathered in April last round the grave of that friend, from whom death had severed him for a time, there was one feeling in many hearts — that they had lost one who, beyond any living person, was in full possession of the whole soul of him to whom death had re-united him — that the most trustworthy, the most intimate, the most continuous of the authorities for the history of Arthur Stanley, had passed into the world beyond the grave, in the person of his friend Hugh Pearson.

He returned to Oxford in the autumn of 1841, and soon after became Lecturer, and in due time Tutor and Dean of his new College, where he resided continuously, or nearly so, till his removal to Canterbury.

This perhaps is the place to speak of his life as an Oxford tutor, the capacity in which I, and many others of his most devoted friends, first knew him. Yet, in speaking to an audience north of the Tweed, there may be some difficulty in bringing before you what that life really was. But you are perhaps aware that until quite lately every Oxford student — though the word

"student" in this technical sense is unknown on the
banks of the Isis — passed three years of his academical life within the walls of one of about a score of Colleges. Of these Colleges — each contained within a
separate, more or less imposing, block of stone-built
buildings, with its own chapel, its own dining-hall, its
own library, its own lecture rooms — the University
practically consisted. Each College was under the
separate government of its own head — Master, War-
den, Provost, Principal, President, as the case might be
— and its own fellows and tutors; and each contained
its own group of undergraduate students. The University, by which all degrees were conferred, was
represented by disciplinary and other authorities, by
examiners, and by professors. But at the time of which
I speak, professorial lectures had, with few exceptions,
fallen into almost entire abeyance; and the instruction
which undergraduates received was given within the
walls of their own College, supplemented often by private tuition from teachers whom they selected at their
will and remunerated from their own resources.

The position, therefore, of a College tutor, living in
rooms among his pupils, waited on by the same servants, attending daily the same chapel services, dining
at the same hour in the same hall, was—may I not say
still is?—one singularly fitted to open a field for usefulness to those who have the rare gift of influencing
young men. Into the duties and opportunities of this
position Stanley threw himself with all the ardour of
his nature, and the impression that he made and the

work which he achieved was, at the time, unexampled.
It can only be understood by those who are familiar
with the influence gained by the almost life-long labours
of his own almost life-long friend, Professor Jowett, now
Vice-Chancellor of the University of Oxford, at a College better known in Edinburgh than that to which
the scholar of Balliol had migrated. As compared with
that friend, Stanley had no doubt some drawbacks as a
tutor. "I am no moral philosopher or metaphysician,"
he said of himself later. His interest in the minuter
shades of philological scholarship was never very keen.
No man knew better his own weak points. But the page
of History, ancient, modern, or sacred, was to him, in the
truest sense of the words, "rich with the spoils of time;"
and he knew how to make that page glow with the
light of wisdom and of poetry, and to aid his pupils to
regard those spoils as very treasures. How well two or
three of us must remember that well-marked Herodotus
which he freely lent us. It had its special marks in
coloured lines to indicate, first, passages noteworthy
for the Greek; secondly, passages bearing on Greek
history, or on the time of Herodotus; thirdly, passages
containing truths for all time. He was already giving
himself to the study of the Old and New Testaments
with an enthusiasm which never left him, and which he
was able to communicate to one after another of those
who came under his influence. Even now there are
those who, in East-end parishes, in country villages,
in far-off Missionary stations, as well as in what are
called the high places of the Church, feel the impulse

which they then received from him. So keen was the
interest inspired by his Divinity lectures, that not
only did we, his pupils, continue to attend them in
the very crisis and agony of our final work for our
degrees, but little by little we obtained permission to
introduce our friends; and the first germ of those
inter-Collegiate lectures which have revolutionised
Oxford teaching, and gave your new professor of
Greek a field to display his masterly gifts as a
teacher, is to be found in those close-packed chairs
that crowded the still damp ground-floor rooms in the
then New Buildings, as they are still called, on the top-
most story of which our lecturer had his rooms. He was
—need I say it?—a singularly attractive and inspiring
teacher; but in saying this I feel that I have said
little. It is impossible for me to describe to you, it
is difficult for me to analyse to myself, the feelings
which he inspired in a circle, small at first, but with
every fresh term widening and extending. The fascination, the charm, the spell, were simply irresistible;
the face, the voice, the manner; the ready sympathy,
the geniality, the freshness, the warmth, the poetry, the refinement, the humour, the mirthfulness and
merriment, the fund of knowledge, the inexhaustible
store of anecdotes and stories, told so vividly, so
dramatically, — I shall not easily enumerate the gifts
which drew us to him with a singular, some of us with
quite a passionate devotion. Arnold, before and after
his death; Arnold, to us Rugby men — well! he was
Arnold still. We never dreamed of a rival to him. I

am sure that in those days we never thought of weigh-
ing Stanley against him. They dwelt apart in our
minds; apart, yet coupled in a sense together. Living
or dead, the Elijah of that day was wrapped to our
young souls in a certain cloud of awe. Stanley himself never quite lost the feeling. But the Elisha on
whom his mantle fell was near and dear to us. That
sympathetic touch that won him to the end of his
life fresh friends at every breath he drew, had already
come to one who as a child had lived much alone, un-
companionable and undemonstrative to a fault, writing
his boyish poems, and hidden in the light of ideas and
knowledge which he was hourly absorbing. It is felt
by some of us, as a thing that coloured our whole lives
from that day to this. We walked with him, sometimes took our meals with him — frugal meals, for he
was at the mercy of an unappreciative college "scout,"
who was not above taking advantage of his master's
helplessness in arranging for a meal, and his indifference to any article of diet other than brown bread
and butter; we talked with him over that bread and
butter with entire freedom, opened our hearts to him;
while his perfect simplicity, no less than his high-bred
refinement, made it impossible to dream that any one
in his sober senses could presume upon his kindness.
He was steeped in work. For two years he was devoting himself to the immortal biography of his
master. Afterwards he was continually studying,
devouring books, entering more and more keenly into
the theological and other controversies of the next few

years, deeply and absorbingly interested, I need hardly
say, in the crisis through which the University and the
Church were passing in the years between 1841 and
1845. He was surrounded more and more by friends
and associates of his own age, or older ; he was becoming more and more conspicuous in literary as well
as in theological circles. He was busied in writing such
sermons as those on the Apostolic Age, in which he
first made his mark as an academical preacher and — I
use the word in its widest and truest sense — as a
theologian. He was full of schemes, full of hopes, for
the reorganisation and enlargement of the University,
as ultimately effected by the Commission of which, in
the closing part of this chapter of his life, he was the
indefatigable Secretary. I remember how, soon after
I had ceased to be his pupil, and had reached the
dignity of a junior Fellowship, on our return from a
walk, in which he had discussed the question of a royal
or parliamentary Commission—a question which could
not have been mentioned in ordinary Oxford society
without causing scandal—he paused for a moment opposite one of the most wealthy, not perhaps the most educational of Colleges, and whispered, "The only drawback
to such reforms is that this institution must at once
flourish on the ruins of Balliol." Reform has come, and
Balliol still holds its own ! But in spite of all these
interests and all these employments, and in spite of a
correspondence that grew with the growing number
of his friendships, and in spite of the weeks which he
almost yearly gave to travel, the amount of his time

and of his best self which he gave to his younger
friends was something almost incredible. Some of us
can recall the half-amusing, half-touching, efforts which
he made to become acquainted with, and win the confidence of, a class of men least likely to be impressible
to one like himself; the missionary spirit, if I may use
the phrase, in which he regarded his relation to the
undergraduates of his College; a College which steadily
continued—owing mainly to his own reputation—to
attract to it an unusual portion of the *élite* of the
best schools in England. Many must still remember
his introducing what had long been abandoned in that
ancient College—I am not sure that he had not to go
back as far as the times of the Commonwealth for a
precedent—the preaching of occasional sermons in the
College chapel. They will recall his very voice, and
accent, and look, and manner, and gesture. But it was
not his preaching, nor his teaching, it was himself most
of all which impressed us. We always knew—and it
was the secret of his winning to the end of his days
the hearts of the young, and, let me add, of the humble
and working classes of his countrymen — we always
knew that he treated us and felt to us as a friend;
cared for us, sympathised with us, gave us his heart,
and not his heart only, but his best gifts; that we did
not sit below the salt, but partook with him of all that
he had to give; and what he gave us was just that
which was most calculated to win and attract, as well
as to inspire and stimulate. There still live in my
own memory the vivid recollections; there have been

placed in my hands the still existing evidences of his
active kindness and beneficence to present or former
pupils; the letters, long or short, of sympathy in
trouble, advice in doubt or difficulty; the pecuniary
aid given so freely and so delicately whenever he saw
an opening to do so with good results.

I have said perhaps, out of the abundance of my
own recollections, with the written testimonies of
others by my side, more than you will have cared to
hear on this chapter of his life; yet it is one which
may have a special interest in the close vicinity of a
great northern University. Let me end by repeating
once more what I have already said, that the impression which he made upon many at least of his Oxford
pupils was one which it is impossible to convey fully
to those outside that circle; it will be intelligible in
some degree to all who have enjoyed his society.
You could not, I may almost say, think of evil in his
presence. The atmosphere round him was as pure
and elevating as it was rich in interest. It was indeed
full of " whatsoever things are pure, whatsoever things
are lovely, whatsoever things are of good report."

I must pass over the effective part that he bore,
towards the close of his residence in Oxford, in introducing, as Secretary to the first University Commission, many changes of the most important and vital
nature in the constitution of the University. To
reform an ancient institution, to breathe new life
into venerable forms, was a work exactly suited to
one as averse from a merely obstructive conservatism

as he was impatient of the spirit that seeks only to destroy. It is enough for one who was a member of a Commission but lately appointed to follow mainly in the lines then laid down, to say that the reforms established were chiefly directed to two objects: first, to widen the influence of the University by the removal of restrictions, local, professional, or theological, which kept more than half closed the admission to its emoluments and its distinctions; and secondly, to revivify an almost dormant Professoriate.

I must pass over, also, the intense interest which then, as always, he took in the contemporary history of his own country and of the Continent. Two instances only let me give. Some here will recall the now distant fall of Sir R. Peel's Ministry in the summer of 1846, after the full establishment of free trade by that great Minister. On that occasion the young tutor of University wrote as follows: — "Peel's speech is, to me, the most affecting public event which I ever remember: no return of Cicero from exile, no triumphal procession up to the temple of Capitoline Jove, no Appius Claudius in the Roman Senate, no Chatham dying in the House of Lords, could have been a truly grander sight than that great Minister retiring from office, giving to the whole world free trade with one hand, and universal peace with the other, and casting under foot," he adds, " the miserable factions which had dethroned him —

'E'en at the base of Pompey's statue,
Which all the while ran blood, great Cæsar fell.'

So I write, the metaphor being suggested by an eye-witness, who told me that it was Mark Antony's speech over Cæsar's body, but spoken by (Cæsar) himself."

Again the shock that passed through Europe in 1848 moved him profoundly. I have no doubt that his journals will be found to contain a perfect magazine of anecdotes of Guizot, Lamartine, Louis Philippe, and the Parisian mob. "Here I am," he writes from London in July of that year, "working hard at I. Corinthians, and seeing no one of importance except Guizot, and two or three more eye- or ear-witnesses of Feb. 24 or June 24, whose accounts I treasure up for my grand-nephews, when they come in 1894, on the outbreak of the Fourth French Revolution and the formation of the Sclavonic Empire, to hear the traditions of the great days of 1848" (July 29th, '49).

Meantime, if the circle of his personal friends, and of his private and public interests, was extending year by year, his public position was becoming every year more prominent and less acceptable to a large portion of the religious world in England, and, I may perhaps add, in Scotland also. Great as was the impression made by the life of Arnold, there was an instinctive feeling that even Arnold's unquestionable hold on the essential truths of Christianity represented another form of religious belief to that on which the views and principles either of the High Church or of the Evangelical party were moulded; and both these parties agreed in regarding his biographer with somewhat of a growing distrust and suspicion. It did not win him the support of the High Church clergy that he had devoted himself heart and soul to prevent the condemnation in the Oxford Convocation of Mr. Ward, who had succeeded Dr. Newman as their acknowledged leader in 1845, or had done his utmost to defeat the formal censure of the celebrated tract No. 90 by the same assembly. They knew well that he had no sympathy with their most cherished views, and the divergence might have been read between the lines of all that he had as yet published, even if he had not met their somewhat exclusive claims to represent the "Church Party" by the assertion that the Church of England was, "by the very conditions of its being, not High, or Low, but Broad."

On the other hand, the leaders of the Evangelical section of English Churchmen were not won to him, but the reverse, by the language in which in 1850 he hailed the then famous "Gorham judgment," the Magna Charta of their continued existence in the Church, in the earliest, but not the least telling or brilliant, of his theological contributions to the "Edinburgh Review." When he spoke of " the inestimable advantage" of that decision as consisting in the fact that "it retained within the pale of the Establishment both the rival schools of Theology," and went on to add that " the Church of England was meant to include, and always had included, opposite and contradictory opinions not only on the point now in dispute, but on other points as important, or more important than this," he seemed to many of those whose cause he was pleading to be

shaking the very basis of the Christian faith. They
would scarcely have been conciliated had they been
told, as they were told twenty years later, that the
main substance of that very Article had been written,
though not published, several years earlier, "in the
hope of averting the catastrophe which drove out from
the Church of England such men as Dr. Newman and
his friends." They felt also that, averse as he might
be to impress upon others ideas of a purely negative
and unsettling character, though he had deprecated
the day of inevitable trial, "when the works of German Biblical criticism would be read indiscriminately
by all the men, women, and children in England,"
yet his views on Scriptural Inspiration, and on other
important subjects, differed widely from their own.

I may have an opportunity further on of saying
something of his theological position. But do not let
me for a moment disguise the fact that however strong
his personal piety, however deep his own religious
convictions, he stood from first to last quite apart from
both the two great parties in the English Church; that
his theological views squared with neither. I do not
know that he himself ever disguised the fact that he
looked on each, even as he said much later of the separate Churches of Christendom, "as having something
which the other had not," and recognised "the human,
imperfect, mixed character" of each. The natural
result was that from first to last he was an object of
almost equal suspicion, an object, theologically speaking, I might almost say, of almost equal antipathy to
both.

When however the time came, in 1851, for him to
leave Oxford and accept the Canonry of Canterbury,
the reception which he met with in his new home was
cordial, and the dissatisfaction, doubtless felt in some
quarters, was expressed in undertones. The change
was well timed. His friends had begun to feel that
the position which he had gained as a student and as a
writer had long merited public recognition. They felt
also that it was time that he should be removed from
the many wearisome details of a College Tutor's life;
and his father's death and his consequent entering
into a moderate amount of landed property had, under
then existing regulations, made the retention of his
Fellowship impossible. Heavy blows indeed had fallen
on that happy family circle. In September of 1849 he
had reached Brahan Castle just in time to see his
father lying unconscious, and passing away from a life
of unwearied labour. In a short time came the news
that in the month previous the youngest son, who had
reached the rank of a captain in the Royal Engineers,
had succumbed to a sudden attack of fever in Van
Diemen's Land. As his young widow entered the
harbour of Sydney in hopes of receiving the support
and consolation of a welcome from her husband's
brother, Captain Owen Stanley, she found that he too
had lived only long enough to hear that both his
brother and his father had gone before. Worn out
with the incessant toil entailed by his survey, in command of the sailing frigate *Rattlesnake*, of the perilous
Coral Sea, and by the intense anxiety attendant on a

lengthened cruise "amongst a mass of shoals and reefs, where the lead gives no warning, and the look-out from the masthead is often useless from the colour of the coral," the gallant sailor, "after twenty-three years of arduous service in every clime," died in March, 1850, at the age of thirty-eight.*

His father's death struck him to the quick. "The crash, the gloom, the uprooting and the void," he wrote between his father's death and funeral, "is at times overwhelming, but of him even more than of Arnold I believe that I shall soon feel that I would not have him back again for all that a restored home could give." And those who knew him well may recognise the occasional reference in later sermons and addresses to that circle of brothers and sisters, each so rich in different gifts, which time and death had so greatly broken up; or knew how vivid was the recollection of the first accumulation of family sorrows on that affectionate heart.

You will not expect me to enter into the details of his life as a Canon of Canterbury. You have heard perhaps of his famous interview, immediately after his nomination, with your great countryman, Thomas Carlyle, and of the answer which he received at last to the twice-repeated question, "What is the advice

---

* Few, perhaps, who saw the remarkable gathering of men of science at the funeral of Arthur Stanley remembered that it was not the least eminent among them, Professor Huxley, who had been his eldest brother's companion in that distant voyage, and who, in the pages of the " Westminster Review," paid a tribute to the memory of his lost friend and commander after his return to England.

which you would give to a Canon of Canterbury?"
" Dearly beloved Roger " (the answer began in jest,
but ended in earnest), " *Whatsoever thy hand findeth
to do, do it with all thy might ;*" and with all his might
he strove, there and elsewhere, to find the right work,
and to do it with his might — strove to realise in
himself a thought he often expressed, not without a
tacit reference to his father's experience as well as to
his own ; " High offices in Church and State may fill
even ordinary men with a force beyond themselves ; "
and again, " Every position in life, great or small,
can be made almost as great or as little as we desire
to make it."

It was, I need not say, delightful for him, in spite of
much natural regret at leaving Oxford friends, not only
to " have leisure for a few tranquil years of independent
research or studious leisure " (I quote his own words,
used later), " where he need contend with no pre-
judices, entangle himself with no party, travel far and
wide over the earth with nothing to check the constant
increase of knowledge which such experience brings ; "
but to be placed at once in connection (to use once
more his own words) " with the cradle of English
Christianity, the seat of the English Primacy," "his
own proud Cathedral," as he learnt to call it, " the
Metropolitan Church of Canterbury."

There can be no doubt that his seven years at Canterbury were seven years of exceeding value to him.
Here it was that he brought to full ripeness and
maturity his wonderful gift of throwing a fresh and

human interest, one which reaches even the most
unlettered of his hearers or readers, into great historic scenes or great historic monuments. It was at
Canterbury that he at once undertook to impress
upon his new fellow citizens the great advantages
which they enjoyed by living under the shadow of
that stately fabric. It was not at Westminster but at
Canterbury that he found his earliest opportunity for
uttering the characteristic words, " It is not too much
to say that if anyone were to go through the various
spots of interest in or around our great Cathedral, and
ask, What happened here? Who was the man whose
tomb we see? Why was he buried here? What effect
did his life and death have upon the world? a real
knowledge of the history of England is to be gained,
such as the mere reading of books or lectures would
utterly fail to supply." *   It was not at Westminster
but at Canterbury that he spoke of " what may seem
to be mere stones or bare walls becoming so many
chapters of English history."   None who ever went
through that grand Cathedral with him will forget
the vividness with which each successive incident
in the tragic story of the murder of Becket was
re-enacted, as it were, on the very spot where each
occurred.   In his " Memorials of Canterbury," dedicated to a venerable brother Canon who still resides
—may he long do so!—in his delightful home in
those beautiful precincts, and written, as he says in
the Introduction, " in intervals of leisure, taken from

* Memorials of Canterbury, p. 99.

subjects of greater importance," he gave to the world
a more than sufficient justification for his removal to
that fair city. But the advantages of his life at Canterbury were not limited to literary work, whether in immediate connection with that life or on other subjects,
such as his "Commentary on the Epistles to the Corinthians," written mostly at Oxford but completed
there. It was here that the freedom which he enjoyed
for gratifying his instinctive love for travel was so fully
indulged, and with such great results. Already, as we
have seen, he had taken every opportunity of "enlarging his mental vision," of seeking a fresh and complete
influx of new ideas, by visiting far and wide scenes and
places of historic interest. Spain, Germany, including
Bohemia, France, and Italy, he had already traversed.
Scotland also, as I have already said, had begun to exer-
cise over him the fascination which became afterwards
so much deeper and stronger. But now he took a wider
flight. After a visit to Italy and Rome with his mother
and two sisters, and after returning to England with hot
haste in time to be present at the funeral of the Duke of
Wellington, he started, at the close of 1852, for the tour
in Egypt and the Holy Land, which resulted in the
publication of, next to the "Life of Arnold," the most
widely popular of all his works, "Sinai and Palestine."
Of the wonderful light which that work throws on
sacred history I shall not now say one word. I will
only say that the greater part of it is but a reproduction
of letters written to his friends. As Professor Goldwin
Smith wrote to him on his return, "You have nothing

to do but to piece together your letters, cut off their
heads and tails, and the book is done." But something
I may say of his journey which was not recorded in the
pages of " Sinai and Palestine." Two of the party of
four were Scotsmen. One of these, from his justice,
good temper, and power of command, received from
their Eastern attendants the name of "the Governor";
but Stanley was invariably "the Sheik," the holy man.
He gained this title partly from his knowledge of the
localities which they visited, and his familiarity with
and interest in all the strange outgrowth of Arab
legends ; but he gained it also by the pure and beautiful, and, in their unsophisticated eyes, unversed in the
bitter controversies of the Christian world, by the
saintly character of one whom they watched and lived
with day and night for weeks. Well can we who
knew the man understand the story, how Mohammed,
the faithful dragoman, after the last farewell was over,
crept down into the cabin, knelt and seized his hand,
and then rushed away with an outburst of passionate
grief at parting with one whom he would never see
again, and whom, in spite of the difference of creed,
he reverenced as a saint. The journey was, notwith-
standing inevitable occasional discomforts, a source to
him of the deepest delight. "Those glorious days," he
said of them, " which can now never be taken away."
At Cairo and on the Nile he re-read the " Arabian
Nights ; " and, what seemed to him, destitute as he was
of his father's taste for birds or beetles, "the infinite,
endless, boundless, monotony" of the voyage up the

Nile was beguiled by reading all the parts of the Bible
that referred to Egypt in the original Hebrew. In the
same spirit he prepared himself for a careful survey of
the sacred soil of Palestine, by toiling through every
word of Robinson's elaborate four volumes. " I read
them," he said, " now riding on the back of a camel in
the desert, now travelling on horseback* through the
hills of Palestine, now under the shadow of my tent
when I came in weary from the day's journey. They
are among the very few books of modern literature
of which I may truly say that I have read every
word." Those who had the privilege of visiting him
at Canterbury on his return, and found him overflowing with the recollections of his journey, as well as
with the intense interest inspired by the Cathedral and
its neighbourhood, will well understand his closing a
letter of invitation to Professor Max Müller with the
words, " I consider I was never so well worth a visit."

It was from Canterbury, also, towards the end of
his tenure of office there, that he made the visit to
the Baltic, St. Petersburg, and Moscow, the result
of which he embodied in his volume on the Greek
Church. " I have been deeply interested," he says in
a letter written in a Baltic steamer on Sept. 29th, 1857,
to one who was becoming every year more closely
united to him by friendship and by sympathy, Mr., or,

---

* He was probably one of the worst horsemen in Europe, Asia, or
Africa, from the day when his first visit to Norwich was marred by a
fall from what he called "the episcopal pony," to the day when his
life was all but lost on his second visit to Egypt with the Prince of
Wales, and a donkey was henceforth found for him.

as here he should be called, for it is to Scotland that he
owes the title, Dr. George Grove, " I have been deeply
interested in Norway and Sweden, more in St. Petersburg, most of all in Moscow. Russia fully answered my
expectations, in the flood of light which I derived from
my sight of those two great cities. If you wished to bring
out the dramatic effect of Russian history, it could not
be better done than by the contrast between Moscow
and Petersburg. The great Eastern nation striving to
become Western, or, rather, the nation half Eastern,
half Western, dragged against its will by one gigantic
genius, literally dragged by the heels and kicked by
the boots of the Giant Peter, into contact with the
European world." I dare not read more, though the
opening passage is barely a fair sample of a letter
every line of which is full of picturesque effects, as he
enumerates the points of Oriental character in the
Russian people — " some great," he says, " some small,
but all delightful to me, as making me feel once more
in the ancient East." Of that ancient East he wrote
on his first visit that he now understood the then
Mr. Disraeli's language, who speaks of it in " Tancred "
as being, to a traveller from Europe, " another planet."

If his residence in Canterbury was not only a
delightful pause in his always busy life, and fruitful
as giving him leisure for such journeys as these, and
for such literary work as his " Memorials of Canterbury," " Sinai and Palestine," and his " Canterbury
Sermons," it was not less delightful or less useful in
developing another and a different side of his character.

It was now that for the first time he exchanged his
bachelor's rooms at Oxford for a house and home of his
own. It is needless to say how often that home was
cheered by the presence of his mother, dearer now to
him, if possible, than ever, or of his sisters, one of
whom had been for some time the wife of his early
friend, Charles Vaughan, then Head Master of Harrow.

Rarely has that ancient city of Southern England
had such a centre of social life within its fair Cathedral
precincts. Citizens and officers, residents in the neighbourhood, visitors from afar, old friends and new
acquaintances, met in that most delightful of homes,
and there it was that the once self-contained and retiring youth, the child shy to the verge of moodiness,
developed those social gifts which made him to the
end of his days not only the coveted guest of every
circle in England—I might almost say in Europe—but
the very best and most delightful of hosts. What
those social gifts were, some here have the happiness
of knowing. Their charm lay in their perfect simplicity and naturalness, in their use being so obviously
based on the kind heart that was bent on one purpose
— to cheer, to amuse, to instruct others, not on self-
display. There come back to the memory of one here,
perhaps of many, times when the most delightful, the
most dramatic and picturesque of his stories were
told with all the charm of his voice and manner—the
voice that became, as has so well been said, "resonant
and full" when he recited a quotation from poetry, or
a saying of interest—not to charm a listening circle of

men or women of mark or rank, but to amuse a weary
and silent friend, or to enliven a tedious drive through
country lanes. I will only add that he himself greatly
enjoyed this first entry into the position of a house-
holder. At the close of his Canterbury life, in a letter
written on the sudden bereavement, by his young wife's
death, of one of his Oxford pupils, he writes with something of a prophetic instinct, " But yet on the whole
I feel sure that even with such dreadful contingencies
in store it is better to have had a home and wife than
never to have had either. To have had even a home
as I have had at Canterbury has been, I am convinced,
an immense step in life — much more would the other
have been."

The great public and national events which marked
this period can only be noticed here so far as they most
closely affected his personal history. It will be enough
to mention his sister's mission to the hospitals of the
Crimea, or rather of Scutari, in the Crimean war; and
in connection with this mission, his own first visit to the
Court of England and to the Queen and Royal family;
his delight in the appointment of his dear friend,
Archibald Campbell Tait, his own tutor at Balliol, and
Arnold's successor at Rugby, to the see of London
(1856). " He will give," he said of the present revered
Primate of England,* " he will, in my humble judg-
ment, give the Church of England a great lift. Scot-

* The words, as well as those on the next page, are printed as
spoken in November. It was on the 3rd of the following month that
the Archbishop died.

land," he adds, "as you may suppose, claps her hands
and sings for joy at his elevation." And well might
Scotland do so! One of the first acts of the new
Bishop of London was to appoint Arthur Stanley as his
examining chaplain, an office which he retained till his
appointment to the Deanery of Westminster, and in
which he was succeeded by the present Bishop of
Durham. Almost greater still was his satisfaction —
greater even than that with which he hailed the appointment to Rugby of Dr. Temple—at the elevation to
the Bishopric of Calcutta of one of whom he once spoke,
"as on the whole the very best Bishop whom he had
ever known," the then Master of Marlborough College,
Dr. Cotton. It is to this dear friend of his that your
countryman and our Primate bore so lately, from that
sick bed which is the centre of so many prayerful
thoughts in England and in Scotland, his testimony
that "he wielded among the civilians of India a
power unknown to any of the great men who have
ever occupied the see."

The year 1858 saw the close of the calm and fruitful
stage in his life's progress, of which Canterbury was the
scene. He was now to enter on a work for the duties
of which his whole life might well have seemed one long
preparation, that of the Professorship of Ecclesiastical
History in the University of Oxford. The appointment
is vested in the Crown, and it may be well to remind you
that each of the three important offices which Arthur
Stanley held in succession came to him from the same
source, and were due to the impression which his genius

and character had made, not on the Church in its
narrowest sense, nor again on the Crown in the personal sense of the term, but on the Church and nation
at large as represented in the "kingly commonwealth
of Great Britain," by the Sovereign and her responsible
Ministers. Which of these three offices he would have
ever held, had the appointment rested in other hands,
was a question which his friends would sometimes ask
with amused perplexity, and answer with much relief
and thankfulness that things were as they were; that
the selection in these cases lay with the First Minister
of the Crown, who was free to give due weight to
claims which were, in the general opinion, unrivalled.
"There is one and one only possible candidate, and
that is Arthur Stanley," were the words of his distinguished friend, the historian Milman, then Dean
of St. Paul's, when consulted on the subject by an
influential Churchman.

I do not suppose that there are many here who have
ever read the three inaugural lectures which he delivered before crowded audiences beneath what I venture
to call the august roof of the Sheldonian Theatre at Oxford. That Theatre had been the scene, one-and-twenty
years before, of his own early distinction as the reciter
of the Prize Poem which to the discerning critic might at
once have revealed the unmistakeable stamp of true
genius. Five years later, in the spring of 1842, it had
been thronged again by crowds, the great majority
of whom came to see, for the first and for the last
time, the striking face and listen to the powerful

voice of one who bore the name, suggestive to many
only of aversion and dread, of Thomas Arnold. And
now, in the place where Arnold, to the joy and exulta-
tion of his devoted pupils, in the last spring given him
on earth, had, by his simple and manly eloquence, won
back the heart of an alienated University, the most
distinguished of those pupils poured forth his accumu-
lated treasures of study, travel, thought, and imagination. The opening words of his first lecture were
eminently characteristic. Years before he had been
struck by a passage in the " Pilgrim's Progress," in
which the pilgrim Christian was cheered and solaced
on his way by the sight of the treasures and records of
the palace of which the name was " Beautiful." He
had promised himself at the time that, should he ever
address an Oxford audience on ecclesiastical history, he
would begin his lecture with the quotation. And he
kept his promise. The first words which he uttered
in his capacity of Professor of Ecclesiastical History
were taken from the great work of the devout nonconformist tinker of Midland England, whom sixteen
years later, when Scotland and Scottish associations
had filled so large a part of the background of that
vivid imagination, he startled a Bedfordshire audience
by speaking of as "the Robert Burns of England."
He closed the last of the three lectures with a quotation from the same author.

Read these Lectures even now, in the light of his
later works and his later letters, and you will see that
they embody his whole views, his whole life, his whole

self. Listen to his characteristic determination to begin
his treatment of his subject, not with the era of the
Reformation, not with the rise of the Papacy, not with
the age of the earlier Fathers, but to start from "the
first dawn of the history of the Church, when in Ur of
the Chaldees the first figure in the long succession that
has never since been broken, the first Father of the
Universal Church, started on that great spiritual migration which from the day that Abraham turned his face
away from the rising of the sun has been stepping
steadily Westward." Read his earnest protest against
the "narrowing and vulgarising process by which the
original sense of great theological terms becomes de-
faced and marred and clipped by the base currency of
the world, till the Christian Church comes to signify,
not the whole congregation of faithful men dispersed
throughout the world, but a priestly caste, a monastic
order, a little sect, or a handful of opinions; till the
word "ecclesiastical" has come down to signify, not the
moral, not even the social or political interests of the
whole community, but the very opposite of these—such
questions as the retention or abolition of a vestment,
its merely outward, accidental, ceremonial machinery."
Read his estimate of the position of great laymen,
such as St. Louis in France, Dante in mediæval Italy,
"the half heretic half Puritan" Milton in England, as
"the true interpreters, the true guides of the thoughts
and feelings of their respective ages." Read his description, drawn from the happy experience of his own past,
and foreshadowing that of his future life, of the effect

of " meeting face to face an opponent whom we have
known only by report. He is different from what we expected ; we cannot resist the pressure of his hand, the
glance of his eye." Read above all the words in which
he pours out his whole soul on that which lay so near
his heart, " the endless vigour and vitality of the words
of Holy Scripture." Read, if you wish to grasp the
key to, I had almost said, his whole lifelong position as
a theologian, the energetic expression which he gives to
what to some may seem an idle dream, but which was
to him the mainstay of his life, the conviction " that in
that virgin mine, the insufficiently explored records,
original records, of Christianity, there are still materials for a new epoch ; that another and a different estimate of the points on which Scripture lays the most
emphatic stress warrants the hope that the existing
materials, principles, doctrines of the Christian religion
are far greater than have ever yet been employed, and
that the Christian Church, if it ever be permitted or
enabled to use them, has a long lease of new life and
new hope before it." I quote the words, because, uttered
in 1858, they contain the very gist of that which, whether you or I, this person or that person, agree or disagree,
was his belief, his hope, his aspiration, now bright, now
sadly clouded, till his dying day. Approve or disap-
prove, call him a dreamer, blame him, condemn him,
if you will, but recognise the fact that in this faith
and this hope — that of a new and greater future for
the Church of Christ — Arthur Stanley lived and died.

The interest which was awakened by the opening lec-

tures of the new Professor was sustained throughout
by the more regular courses which they inaugurated.
Those who are familiar with the two first volumes of
his " Jewish Church " will readily understand the at-
traction which they must have had, as spoken lectures,
for the young students of theology, to the majority
of whom they came almost as a new revelation of the
wealth of historical and other teaching that was to be
gathered from the records of Jewish History.   There
were those among them whose subsequent theological
position and tenets differed widely from those of their
gifted teacher ; but not the least emphatic testimony
to the value and the permanent effect on their own
minds of the light thrown by him on the pages of the
Old Testament would be borne by those who could
not possibly be claimed as his theological adherents.

And the mere preparation and delivery of those inspiring and instructive Lectures formed but a small
part of the duties which he set himself to perform.
His old love for the society of the young was rekin-
dled at the sight of the hundreds of undergraduates
swarming in the streets of Oxford. " My heart leaps
up," he would say, repeating a parody suggested by
his friend Clough, "when I behold an undergraduate;"
and it may well be said that to the very end of his days
his years were " bound each to each by the natural
piety " of affection for friends of every age, from early
youth to the latest stage of human life.   It was not
only to the younger members of Christ Church, or to
those who attended his own lectures, that his house

was open. More than one or two of the masters of great
English schools were encouraged to introduce to him
their pupils on their entrance at the University, and,
among those who still mourn his loss most keenly, are
some whose long and close friendship began in this way.

But his social position at Oxford was one as peculiar
and unparalleled as was his own personality. Never
I suppose before, and certainly never since, has there
been a house in which the representatives of the
most opposite views and parties, accustomed to regard
each other as almost belonging to different worlds,
could be won to meet in such free and social intercourse. It was his delight to place side by side at his
table, and to unite in friendly conversation, men who
had hitherto met each other, if at all, only in sharp,
and sometimes acrimonious, debate. And his own
unrivalled social gifts, his humour, his vivacity, his
endless store of anecdotes connected with places and
persons visited in his travels, gave a charm to his society which few, either then or later on at Westminster,
could wholly resist. " What an element," says Bishop
Cotton, in a letter written from Oxford, " of peace
and goodwill is Stanley! so heterogeneous a dinner!
yet all most humorous and cheerful! Stanley's stories about Becket's brains, and Louis XVI.'s blood,
assume a positively sacred colour when they bind
together in friendly union the latitudinarian ——
and the stiff-necked ——." As every year added to
the circle of his friends and acquaintances at a distance, Oxford society was continually enlivened and

diversified by the visits of distinguished foreigners, or persons eminent elsewhere in the fields of literature or science. Whatever storms might rage in academical society, the future guardian of the " great temple of reconciliation and peace " made it his aim to make his own house a place at the threshold of which the demon of controversial bitterness must be exchanged for a more Christian spirit.

Yet the air around him was charged with controversy. One that raged through a great part of his Oxford residence was the question of providing a higher salary than £40 a year for his attached and early friend, the eminent scholar who held, and still adorns, the post of Professor of Greek at that wealthy University. Those whom I am addressing may find it difficult to realise the animosity with which so obvious an act of policy as well as of justice was defeated, time after time, by the votes of theological opponents, or the almost "judicial blindness" by which the seeds of a bitter and rankling sense of injustice, fruitful, alas! of evil to come, were sown broadcast, in the name of a religion of righteousness and peace, among the future leaders of academical life. But it will not be difficult for you to understand or to recall the whirlwind which was raised by the publication, or rather by the attacks and discussion which followed in due time the publication, in 1860, of the famous volume of " Essays and Reviews." It is not my purpose to enter into the details of that long and bitter controversy which for a time convulsed the English

Church, and which was not finally laid to sleep till after
at least three years of clamorous agitation. Stanley's
position was characteristic. He objected most strongly
to the whole scheme and form of the work. "In a com-
posite publication" he recognised from the very first
"a decided blunder." But this was not all. While
admitting that almost the whole of the first, and much
in the last, of the seven Essays, was eminently con-
servative, he censured strongly the generally negative
character of the volume. "No book," he said, "which
treats of religious questions can hope to make its
way to the heart of the English nation, unless it
gives at the same time that it takes away, builds up
at the same time that it destroys." And in addition
to this, he thought that one at least of the Essays
might be fairly charged with "needlessly throwing
before the English public, which had never heard of
them, conclusions arrived at by the lifelong labours
of a great German theologian, without any argument
to support or recommend them. We do not," he
said, "defend the madness of the bull, but we must
bestow some of our indignation on the man who
shakes the red flag in his face." But this felt and
said, he flung himself with all his own generosity and
ardour into the defence of writers who represented,
with whatever drawbacks, the sacred cause, as he
held it, of liberty of thought among the English
clergy, the cause which in the judicial suits which
followed he believed "to be pleading for its very life."
Nowhere has he written with greater force, vivacity,

and energy than in the appeals which he made to the
educated public through the pages of the Edinburgh
Review, in articles written on this question — one
when the storm was at its height, two others when
the danger was past. For he felt himself to be pleading
for a cause which he believed to involve the whole future of the National Church, "the learning of the most
learned, the freedom of the freest, the reason of the
most rational Church in the world." And he dreaded
above all things a breach between the higher intelligence of the rising generation and the tenets of that
Church, which would not only "have dealt a heavy
blow to all biblical study, but have gone far to reduce
it to the level of an illiterate sect or of a mere satellite
of the Church of Rome." By this controversy the
combative side of his nature, which was no less real
if less strongly marked than its peaceful and social
side, was called into full activity, never again to be
allowed an entire repose — I might almost say for the
rest of his life, whether at Oxford or at Westminster.

It was during his residence as Professor at Oxford
that in pursuance of the wish of the lamented Prince
Consort, and at the express desire of the Queen, he accompanied the heir to the throne, in the spring of 1862,
on a second visit to Egypt and Palestine. His old and
curious objection to re-visiting scenes of former travel
had become greatly modified, as that ardent traveller
found that he would soon have to sigh for new worlds
to conquer; and he accepted without hesitation, and
discharged with much real enjoyment, the important

trust committed to him by the Crown. For any sacrifices which it involved he had a rich reward in the additional facilities which he enjoyed, in virtue of the respect paid to his Royal companion, for visiting at last such an object of interest as the Mosque at Hebron. He was repaid still more by the warm feelings which he inspired during those memorable four months in the new circle in which he travelled, alike in the youthful Prince, and in one who bore a name dear to every Scotsman, in General Bruce, the Prince's faithful friend and counsellor, the brother of her who was ere long to be the solace of his life. Sunday, too, after Sunday he was enabled — now on the Nile itself, now in the great hall of the temple at Karnak, " in the grandest building," as he called it, " which the old world ever raised for worship; " now on shipboard at the ancient Joppa, now under canvas above Shechem, or by the springs of Nazareth, or on an Easter morning by the Sea of Tiberias, or "on the way to Damascus," or under the shadow of the temple of Baalbec, or of the cedars of Lebanon, or off the shore of Patmos, to give utterance to the thoughts which such scenes awoke within him. Those short sermons, perhaps more than anything which he ever wrote, reproduce his very inmost feelings on life and death, and on the relation of the human soul to duty and to God.

On one such occasion an event which cast a deep shadow over that otherwise happy journey gave an additional pathos and impressiveness to his words. The news of his mother's death, on Ash Wednesday, 1862, reached him when on the Nile, between Alexandria and Cairo. He preached on the following Sunday, in the neighbourhood of Memphis, a sermon on the lesson for the day, the story of the re-union of Joseph and his brethren in Egypt; a sermon which, for the pathetic eloquence in which it dwells on the sacredness of home, and for the suppressed tenderness and emotion with which its sentences seem to thrill and tremble, has hardly been surpassed in the English language. There is not a word of direct allusion to his own loss, and I have heard that his voice, though deeper than usual, never faltered throughout. But it must have been hard to have listened unmoved to a fellow traveller who had already endeared himself to all his companions in that memorable journey, as he spoke in the presence of the young heir to the throne, still in mourning for his father, of the " ties that link those who have passed into the world beyond the grave, with those to whom their wishes are now commands, their lightest desires sacred wishes, the very mention and thought of whose names draws us upward and homeward," or to the concluding words in which he spoke of "that last best home where Jacob and his sons, Rachel and her children, shall meet to part no more.' *

---

* Till another, and even sadder Ash Wednesday, came to end twelve years of married happiness, he always spoke of his mother's death as the great sorrow of his life, of his mother's character as the best human manifestation to him of the Christian life. He joins the two days together in lines written shortly before his own end. They begin with the words:

"O day of ashes, twice for me
Thy mournful title thou hast earned;

Those who have ever glanced at, still more those
to whom it has been a work of sadness dashed with
delight, to read, after his death, those "Sermons in
the East," will understand his words written after his
return : "My sermons were to me an immense relief,
and it was a great satisfaction to feel that by the
end of the time I had said almost everything that I
could have wished to say." Later on, speaking to one
of his many friends and helpers in Westminster, he
said that his fullest and deepest convictions were,
he thought, to be found in the pages of that volume.

His return to a home now vacant of the mother who
for years had been more than a mother to that loving
son, was necessarily a time of sadness and trial. By
the kind forethought of Her in whose service he had
been absent "o'er seas and deserts far apart," when the
blow fell, and who from that time counted, we may well
believe, his loyal friendship as among the best jewels
in her crown, his first meeting with the sister who so
keenly shared his sorrow took place neither in their
London nor their Oxford home, but under the Royal
roof of Windsor. But the wound was very deep.
He felt in his own words that the "guardian genius"
had "passed away that nursed his very mind and
heart." Twelve months later, in thanking a much-
valued friend for well-deserved words of praise, "You

> For twice my life of life by thee
> Has been to dust and ashes turned."

They end with the words:

> "The secret of a better life
> Read by my mother and my wife."

know," he said, "how what you have said would have
delighted one who is not here to read it. When I think
of this the tears fill my eyes ;" and those to whom his
happiness was dear began to ask each other whether
there was any hope of the vacant place being filled by a
wife worthy of such a husband. Meantime another loss
had saddened him. His new friend and fellow traveller,
General Bruce, the one among the group to whom
he had opened freely all his feelings on his mother's
loss, was taken away after a short illness. Arthur
Stanley was with him when he died, and went to
Scotland to lay him in his grave at Dunfermline.
The friend who saw him on his return will never
forget the conversation. "It was," said Stanley,
"the very first time that I had seen a human soul
pass with full consciousness from this world to the
world beyond." He spoke of the "identity of character remaining to the very last; thoughtfulness for
the absent, consideration and courtesy for others —
no mere outward mask, but shown in his very dying
moments, when the last prayer had been breathed,
to the nurse who attended him. His last farewell
seemed waved to me from the invisible world."

But he had much to call away his mind from private
troubles. The storm raised by " Essays and Reviews "
was still at its fiercest. So also was the controversy
as to the Greek Professorship, of which I have already
spoken. The second volume of Bishop Colenso's
startling work appeared in the same year. The position of one whom he so loved and reverenced as the

saintly Frederick Maurice, was being rendered almost
intolerable by the assaults of those who have, let us
hope, long since repented of the course they took.
Oxford society was divided as it had not been for many
years by bitter controversy. Even his own rare sweet-
ness and gentle charm could not allay all feuds. Even
in the circle of his friends there had been some passing
coolness, and before he quitted Oxford the feelings and
language of some of his theological opponents had
become exceedingly embittered; "so entirely," he
wrote of one of them, "is he, in this respect, bereft
of reason as to render charity comparatively easy."
Yet he disclaimed all wish to leave Oxford. "I
earnestly desire," he said, "a few months of leisure
to consider the events of this last year."

Early, however, in 1863 he took up his pen. Encouraged by an Episcopal Charge delivered to his
clergy by the Bishop of London, his chaplain addressed to him a letter on the terms of Subscription enforced at the Universities and on the clergy.
Nothing can be more telling than the arguments in
which he advocates a careful re-consideration of the
whole question. He points out that the stringent
form then required could only be subscribed as in-
volving a general, not a particular assent; that so understood, there was no section of the English Church,
lay or clerical, which might not innocently accept it.
But he saw also that it was in the power of any
"malignant or narrow-minded partisan" to "rattle
up," as he said, "the sleeping lions, heedless of the

reflection that when aroused, they will devour with
equal indiscrimination on the right hand, and on the
left, and so add to the general evils of controversy
the great and peculiar aggravations of constant im-
putations of dishonesty and bad faith." He pressed
above all on the notice of a Prelate who lived to be
recognised as the wisest and most statesmanlike of
our English Archbishops, that in this direction was
to be sought not the sole, but one, remedy for "the
greatest of all calamities to the Church of England,
the gradual falling off in the supply of the intelli-
gent, thoughtful, and highly educated young men,
who twenty and thirty years ago were to be found
at every Ordination." I must not attempt to carry
the attention of a Scottish audience through a narrative of all that followed; though the results were
great, and the whole question is one of interest not
confined to the Church of England. It is enough
to say that in 1865, after a stout resistance on the
part of those who declared at one time that no re-
laxations were necessary, and at another that any
relaxation would be an act of treason, an Act of
Parliament, following the recommendations of a Royal
Commission, abolished the elaborate subscriptions of
" Assent and Consent to all and everything contained
in the Prayer Book and Articles," and substituted a
simple assent to them, and to the doctrine therein
contained, and a pledge to use these Formularies, and
none other, without lawful authority. The change
was effected with an ease that forms a marked con-

trast to the keen opposition which a movement in
the same direction encountered in the House of Lords
exactly twenty-five years earlier.   Then a petition
from forty clergymen and laymen in behalf of some
modification of the terms of subscription, presented
almost with apologies by Archbishop Whately, and
gallantly supported by Bishop Stanley, had been
almost spurned from the door of the same House, in
which a healing measure was now passed without
opposition, and almost without comment.

CHAPTER III.

(From 1863 to 1881.)

WESTMINSTER.

LATE in the autumn of 1863 came the removal
of Arthur Stanley from Oxford and his appointment to the Deanery of Westminster. At the end
of the same year, postponed somewhat by the un-
easiness caused by Lord Elgin's failing health, came
the great event of his life, his marriage with her
who once more brought sunshine into his heart.

He bade farewell to the University in a sermon
preached in the month of November in the Cathedral
of Christ Church. Nine years were to pass before
that eloquent voice was to be heard again in the
University pulpit. His text was the verse in the
Gospel of St. Luke which describes our Lord as
pausing on the ridge of the Mount of Olives, "the
one absolutely authentic spot in Palestine where
we can say with entire certainty that His presence
passed," to utter, with weeping, the memorable words,
"*If thou hadst known, even thou at least in this thy
day, the things which belong unto thy peace.*" He

threw his whole soul into his parting words. As he spoke of " the grief, the emotion, which stirs our inmost souls at the thought of passing from a great institution of which we have formed a part, with which some of our happiest days have been interwoven," all felt how genuine was that grief, how deep that emotion. But from the beginning to the end there is scarcely a sentence, scarcely a line which does not " thrill and tingle " with warnings and encouragements, aspirations and regrets, rebukes and appeals. The very inmost history of past and recent academical progress and controversies can be read between its lines; the whole history also of the hopes and fears that divided his own breast as he put before his hearers, many of whom he was addressing for the last time, now the possibility of reading in the future " nothing but a dreary winter of unbelief, which is to be the beginning of the end, and to shrivel up every particle of spiritual life; " now, " the danger to the Church of England of losing for ever the noble ambition that faith and freedom, truth and goodness may yet be reconciled; " now, " the glorious prospect to be spoken of — if never hereafter in this place, yet in other spheres, if God so please, and before other hearers so long as life and strength shall last — the glorious prospect to be found in the conviction that in the religion of Christ, better and better understood, in the mind and words and work of Christ, more and more fully perceived, lies the best security. . . . for the things which belong, not to our peace only, but to the peace of

universal Christendom." It would be impossible here
to give any adequate idea of a sermon whose special
interest was, after all, academical. Had any passing
visitor from Scotland found a seat in that crowded
cathedral, he might have recognised an allusion to
Lord Elgin's illness, the news of which had reached
his future brother-in-law on the evening before; he
would have been struck by the recital of some remarkable words of Dr. Chalmers, spoken twenty
years earlier in the High Street of Oxford; he would
certainly have found many to agree with him in
thinking that the most touching passage in that eloquent sermon was the tribute paid to the "blame-
less holy life" of a young Scottish tutor of Christ
Church, who had passed from the Edinburgh Academy
through the University of Glasgow to Balliol, the
news of whose untimely death had reached the
preacher "through yet darker shadows far, far away,"
almost by the same post that had brought the tidings
of his mother's death.

In due time he and Lady Augusta were established
in their home at Westminster. In the prominent yet
absolutely independent position which he had now
reached, many of his friends saw the post most calculated to give to such powers and such a character as
his their full development and influence. It would be
ungracious to recall the public protest raised against
his appointment by one of the most respected and
most learned of the Canons of Westminster, now a
Bishop of apostolic zeal and saintly character, were it

not for the sake of adding that the new Dean at once
showed, as again and again to the end of his days,
that he was filled with that Christian grace that
" thinketh no evil, is not easily provoked," and that
he succeeded ere long in establishing a personal rela-
tionship of cordial and friendly intercourse between
himself and his protesting Canon. But, I may add
that there were some few among his friends who, on
quite other grounds, felt misgivings at his exchange
of an academic office for the wear and tear of the
social and political life of London. Some also, in the
spirit of a saying of Cardinal Newman's — " Universities are the natural centres of intellectual move-
ments," — doubted whether the extended influence
which he was sure to gain over a larger circle would
compensate for the loss of that growing hold on the
minds of the future clergy which his post at Oxford
was yearly ensuring him. The second question is
one that may even now be raised and discussed by
those interested in the life of the University and of
the English Church: to the first, his life at Westminster, so rich in fruitful work and marked results,
is the best reply.

I come now to a difficult question. How can I best
describe that period in his life which extends from the
beginning of 1864 — he was installed on the 9th of
January — to the sad day in July, 1881, when he was
taken from us ? Shall I speak to you of his social
life ? or of his work as Dean ? or of his literary work ?
or speak of him as preacher, or lecturer, or speaker ?

or as plunged in controversy, as the leader in every
movement to promote, in the language of the ancient
instrument to which he declared his assent on his installation, "the enlargement of the Christian Church"?
or, not less, as the champion of all and every one
whom he looked on as the victims of intolerance or
persecution? Or shall I speak to you of his personal
history, his domestic life, its sacred joys and sacred
sorrows? or of his happy autumns spent in your own
country, his frequent visits to this very city? or of his
many sojourns in foreign countries, his extended acquaintance with the most eminent men in Europe?
or of his ever growing circle of devoted friends? or
of the place he held in the affection of the working
classes? — in the more than regard of his Sovereign
and her Family?

As we think of all these things, we think once more
of the irreparable gap which his loss has made, and of
the impossibility of doing adequate justice to such a
subject under close limitations of space or time. If
a few scattered observations can be read or listened to
with attention, what will be the surpassing interest
of the biography of one in whose character his friends
may proudly feel that there is nothing to soften,
nothing to keep back, when all that wealth of materials, of which I have scarcely laid my hand upon a
hundredth part, has been brought before us by a biographer worthy of the task?

For his social life, then, using the term in its widest
sense, let me speak first of the new feature in that life —

CHAP. III.]   *ARTHUR PENRHYN STANLEY.*   99

his marriage, and all that it brought to him. If there
was any apprehension among his earlier friends that
his union with one whom he had met in the circle of
a Court, and who was herself rich in a wealth of friendships, would in any way close the door of his house or
his heart to those to whom they had hitherto stood
open, the fear was soon dissipated. In that gracious
and graceful lady they found a new friend, who gave
no mere lip-welcome to his and her new home. They
rejoiced to see her seated with her own papers and
correspondence in the lofty library, looking westward
into Dean's Yard, which will so long be associated in
many minds with their united memory. It cheered
her to receive on her death-bed twelve years later
the assurance of their gratitude; it rejoiced him
as he sat by her coffin side with one who had shared
those first misgivings, to hear the assurance once more
repeated.

Her usual seat was at a table where, after her death,
stood her bust in marble, a few feet from where her
husband stood at his desk, plying his daily task of
Jewish history, or sermon, or lecture, or article, or
letters, yet ever ready to turn aside for a few moments'
conversation or rest, and then to resume his work where
he had left it. His old pupils marked with an amused
delight her tender care for the health and comfort of
one curiously incapable of taking care of himself, even
in the most essential points of food and dress. And
she not only shared his friendships, but went with
him heart and soul in all his work and all his aspira-

tions, "in every joy and every struggle," * and her
companionship developed in him to the utmost that
capacity for social life in its highest aspect, on which
I have already touched. The Deanery soon became
a social centre as unique of its kind as was its master.
Church dignitaries—not seldom some who half an
hour before, in the presence of Convocation sitting
within ten yards of the room and beneath the same
roof, had denounced their host in terms which have
long been banished from all language but that of theological controversy—felt the spell of those cordial in-
vitations and that genial welcome, and returned from
that plain luncheon-table softened in heart,if not wholly
reconciled to their entertainer. There the Nonconformist minister found that full social recognition, the
absence of which has done much to widen the gulf
between the Church and the Nonconformist world.
There the pioneers of Science found a listener always
appreciative, always eager for information, "keen as
a hound in the pursuit of knowledge," "possessed by
what the French called *la grande curiosité*," full himself to overflowing of a knowledge other than their
own, never depreciating studies which were alien to
the bent of his own genius, never afraid of Truth, always ready to welcome all who sought for her. There
the leaders of literature met on equal terms with a
master of their craft. There too, that high-born chivalry which marked his inmost nature, threw open the

* The words used by himself in his dedication to her memory of
Vol. 3 of his Lectures on the Jewish Church.

doors of that coveted resort to men from whom others
in his position might have withheld a welcome : to the
conscientious, if mistaken, sufferer from theological
bitterness, or to the most eloquent of French priests
who, in the supreme moment when others withdrew
their protest, had dared to beard the Vatican, to question Papal Infallibility, and to assert the right of a
minister of the Catholic Church to Christian matri-
mony. Foreign ecclesiastics, Archimandrites, Bishops
of the Greek Church, met there the representatives of
the American Churches or of Indian Missions. There
too, above all, the class who lived by daily and weekly
wages found a welcome, not merely to the Abbey
monuments, round which he delighted to conduct them
on their Saturday half-holidays, but to what must have
seemed to them the spacious rooms of the quaint and
interesting abode of the Abbots and Deans of Westminster that was now his home. His social gifts, his
stores of anecdotes, his quick perception alike of the
serious and of the ridiculous, his ready sympathy, his
power of apt quotation, are as impossible to describe
as the marvellously expressive countenance, " the eye
now beaming with sympathy " — I quote a Scotsman's
eloquent words — " now twinkling with humour, the
mobile mouth with its patrician curves, and the delicately sensitive face." The remembrance is a possession which those who have enjoyed will never lose, but
which they cannot impart to others. I lighted just now
by chance on a page in the memoir of a lady once well
known here, who in extreme old age received from him

a visit in her retirement among the English lakes: "There is no one like Arthur Stanley," wrote Mrs. Fletcher; "there is no one like Arthur Stanley" is the echo that might have passed from lip to lip through Scotland as through England. And it was not merely that he amused, entertained or instructed. He won hearts. Some of those who would almost have given their own lives to prolong his, had never seen him till he had reached threescore years, and fresh friends clustered round him to the last, ready to toil for him in all good works, not least in the service of the Abbey which he loved.

And yet it must also be stated that he lived in an atmosphere, if on one side of peace, on another of contention and struggle, and that something of the bitterness which, as he sadly said on leaving Oxford, "poisoned the upper springs of academical life," was to be found even in the freer and larger world of London.

It was scarcely to be wondered at. His aims were distinct and clear; and they were not those which were palatable either to the religious world at large or, above all, to his clerical brethren. And he never, as you in Scotland well know, concealed his views, or hesitated, whether among friends or foes, to plead the cause which he had most at heart — "the enlargement," in his own favourite words, "of the Church, and the triumph of all Truth." Every attempt to repress freedom of inquiry within the Church, or to vilify scientific inquiries outside its borders, or to assert the claims of the clergy to resist or to evade the supremacy of law,

found in him the most uncompromising of opponents.
Every effort to widen the borders of the Church,
whether by relaxing a stringent subscription, or by
admitting those whom he called "the nonconform-
ing members of the Church," to every privilege that
the widest interpretation of the law permitted, found
in him a never-failing advocate. His own intense
belief in the paramount importance of the spiritual
and the moral side alike of Christianity and of human
nature, made him somewhat impatient of what he called
"the materialism of the Altar and the Sacristy." His
avowed sympathy with the "far-sighted reformer of
Zurich" in his teaching that "the significance of sacred
rites consists not in the perishable accidents of their
outward token, or in the precise forms of their ministra-
tion, but in the souls and spirits of their receivers," was
perhaps less shócking to those who looked on Zwinglius
as a heretic than his characterising, before the clergy
assembled in Convocation, the vestment controversy,
then and still convulsing many congregations, as a
mere question of "Clergymen's clothes." If it is quite
true that — I quote once more Scottish testimony —
"he stood higher in the respect and affection of a larger
and more varied circle of members of many churches
than any ecclesiastic in the world," it is equally true
that, within his own Church, he shocked and pained
some whom he would fain have won, and was more
fiercely vituperated, and regarded with greater aversion than perhaps any living clergyman, by others
whose partisanship, or sensitiveness to theological dif-

ferences, was too strong for their charity.   Of his defence of the writers of " Essays and Reviews " I have
already spoken.   The strife became even hotter after
his removal to London.   After judgment had been given
by the highest court in favour of the side which he had
espoused, he dashed with one final charge into the fray
to do battle with the Memorial signed by eleven thou-
sand of the clergy against the acquittal which had
been won.   In Convocation, that is, in the assembly
of the Clergy of the Province of Canterbury held at
Westminster, he developed powers of debate the
existence of which neither friends nor foes, nor he
himself had ever suspected.   And those powers he
used freely.   The year 1872 introduced a fresh subject of religious controversy.   An attempt was made
to alter a word in the Rubric that heads the Athanasian Creed, the result of which would have been to
make the reading of that Creed and of the so-called
" damnatory clauses " which it includes, optional in-
stead of obligatory.   The course indicated was supported not merely by its actual leader and inaugurator
the Dean of Westminster, but also by many sober and
influential churchmen.   I am not, I hope, wronging our
venerable Primate in expressing a belief that his judgment, together with that of a considerable portion of the
bench of Bishops — was not wholly unfavourable to
the proposal.   But the strife was perhaps hotter and
keener than any one of the many controversies in
which our friend was involved.   Already he had been
fiercely impugned for including Dissenters from the

Church of England, and among those dissenters a Unitarian, in an invitation to a Celebration of the Holy Communion to be held in Westminster Abbey, which was sent to all the revisers of the Old and New Testament Version. He was looked on as sharing in some way the responsibility incurred by the Primate and the other English Bishops who declined to use the occasion of the meeting of the Pan-Anglican synod for the purpose of confirming the sentence passed by the Bishop of Cape Town on the Bishop of Natal. It is perhaps, therefore, not surprising that his speech in Convocation on the Athanasian Creed was received with some approach to clamorous interruption. Archdeacon after archdeacon rose to protest. One, himself but lately the defendant in an ecclesiastical trial, after a vain appeal to the Prolocutor to silence the audacious speaker, left the meeting in disgust. The words " Great interruption," cries of " No ! no " occur thickly in the report of the proceedings. Hostile pamphlets, printed sermons, fell in showers upon him. His conduct was stigmatised by one church dignitary, whose kindliness of heart is often belied by his unmeasured words, in pages dedicated "by his afflicted servant and much injured son in Christ" to the Archbishop of Canterbury (himself addressed in that dedication with thinly veiled reproaches), as scarcely reconcilable with the most fundamental principles of morality. He and his supporters were warned that "had they conducted themselves in the service of an earthly sovereign with like profligacy, they would inevitably have been tried

by court-martial and shot." They were called upon,
and the call included a host of the most faithful and devoted of the middle party among English Churchmen,
"to go out instantly from the Church of which such
men proclaim themselves disaffected and disloyal ministers." If one of his opponents ended a printed letter with a grateful acknowledgment of "that reverent
love for the Bible which you taught me at Oxford;"
others had recourse to such phrases as "moral de-
pravity," "immoral priests," "traitors in the camp."
He was publicly taunted with committing a graver
offence than "the tutor who corrupts his pupil's mind,
or the trustee who robs the widow and the orphan of
their property." And his opponents were not content
to beat the air with harmless clamour. Such clamour
never ruffled him. But a blow was aimed by once
friendly hands which, had it struck its mark, would
have wounded him to the quick. An organised
effort was made to employ a dormant power of the
Convocation of Oxford for the purpose of erasing his
name from the list of University Preachers in which it
had at last, nine years after his last sermon preached
there, been inserted by the Board charged with the
duty of selection. But so studied an insult to one so
widely honoured was resented by many who were little
accustomed to take part in University controversies.
Even the leaders of the dominant religious party,
though they took no overt step to restrain their fol-
lowers, declined to aid them with their votes; and
the only result of the threatened stigma was to effect

what all but the blindest leaders of the blind might
have easily foreseen, to win him hearty sympathy
and tenfold attention from all that was generous in
youthful Oxford.

I only revive these unpleasing memories in order
to make it clear that he was to the very end of his
life engaged not merely in peaceful study, or in such
calm statements of his views as were embodied in his
utterances here and elsewhere, north of the Tweed
or south, on this side of the Atlantic or the other,
but in a succession of conflicts — that he was the object, not merely of devoted affection and widespread
sympathy, but of exceedingly bitter and undisguised
hostility.

Let me give an instance, or rather three instances of
the manner in which, with a courage and promptitude
of which his early youth gave little promise, but which
was developed in him more and more as life went on,
he was every year more eager to spring to the rescue of
the solitary or the unfriended — more ready to stand
face to face before an excited and hostile majority.
All three shall be taken from his defence of Bishop
Colenso, who had been condemned of heresy by his
Metropolitan the Bishop of Capetown. I choose this
controversy not because it will be a specially welcome or acceptable topic to those whom I address.
It is perhaps the one in which he stood, I will not say
alone, but with less sympathy and less following than
in any other — he never looked behind to see who
followed him. But I choose it because it is most

illustrative of his chivalry and fearlessness, and throws most light on the hostility which he provoked.

I choose it also because he felt and expressed not only a want of sympathy with, but an actual aversion for, the special mode in which the Old Testament was treated in some at least of Bishop Colenso's writings. The object of much of those works was, it seemed, to break down a supposed belief in the literal inspiration of every word of Holy Scripture by invalidating the accuracy of the details of the Old Testament narrative. The aim of Stanley was entirely different—always and invariably to bring out the treasures of the Bible, historical, poetical, moral, spiritual. But though he felt no sympathy with the form which Dr. Colenso's work took, he felt entire sympathy with him as a real and honest searcher after truth; he earnestly desired to protect the Colonial clergy from being "judged by irresponsible Metropolitans by other laws than those of England;" and he strove, in the interests as he believed of truth and freedom, to avert the severance of the Colonial Churches from the State of England.

On the first occasion, so early as 1866, he felt called on at a moment's notice to oppose a resolution brought forward in Convocation, which virtually treated the See of Natal as vacant. After going seriatim through the various points on which Bishop Colenso had been found guilty of heresy by his Metropolitan, and pointing out that in each separate case the condemnation must be shared, sometimes "by sainted Fathers of the Church," sometimes "by English divines and Bishops of unquestioned orthodoxy," sometimes by "hundreds, nay thousands of the English clergy," he ended by challenging, in a very striking passage, those whom he addressed, to institute proceedings against one who, " though on some of these awful and mysterious questions he has expressed no opinion, yet holds the same principles as those which have been condemned by the Bishop of Capetown. That individual is the one who now addresses you. Judge," he said, " righteous judgment." It is needless to say that the challenge was not taken up.

Years after, on an occasion when the death of the Bishop of Capetown was calling forth well merited expressions of sorrow on the part of the Clergy assembled in Convocation, the Dean of Westminster rose and read an extract from a sermon of the Bishop of Natal containing a dignified and affectionate tribute to his work and character. "For myself," Dean Stanley went on to say, " I do not profess to express full agreement with the Bishop's words. To some here they may appear too highly coloured by the recollections of early friendship. But they are a testimony, alike to the Bishop of Capetown, who could inspire such sentiments, and to the Bishop of Natal who could give utterance to them. When the first Missionary Bishop of Africa who translated the Bible into the language of the natives, shall be called to his rest, I trust that there will be found some Prelate presiding over the See of Capetown just and generous enough to render the like homage to the Bishop of Natal."

Lastly, in the midst of a stormy and almost tumultuous scene at a meeting of the venerable Society for the Propagation of the Gospel, in the early part of the year before that in which he died, he once more stood forth as the solitary and undaunted champion of one for whom he had pleaded years before as "absent, friendless, unpopular," "as attacked by every epithet which the English language has been able to furnish against him." "The Bishop of Natal," he said, "is the one Colonial Bishop who has translated the Bible into the language of the natives of his diocese. He is the one Colonial Bishop who, when he believed a native to be wronged, left his diocese, journeyed to London, and never rested till he had procured the reversal of that wrong. He is the one Colonial Bishop who, as soon as he had done this, returned immediately to his diocese and his work. For these acts he has never received any praise, any encouragement from this the oldest of our Missionary Societies. For these deeds he will be remembered when you who censure him are dead, buried, and forgotten."

It was surely not without reason that one of your own foremost Divines spoke of him as "the champion of the vilified name, the lost cause."

Let me pass on now to his official life as Dean of Westminster. How deep, how intense was his interest in the venerable fabric committed to his care, I need not say. Within three years of his appointment he had completed, incredible as it may appear, his "Memorials of Westminster Abbey." To that thick volume,

crowded with information of every kind, men of slower
powers of work might have devoted half their lives.
It is a full guide to all the treasures of that vast historical museum. It is deficient only on the architectu-
ral side, for of architecture he would sometimes plead
as entire ignorance as of music. But with all the ac-
cumulated knowledge ready for him in existing works,
and with all the help gladly given him by friendly
hands and heads, it is a really prodigious work. He
himself spoke lightly of it. Its very diffuseness of
aim, and its encyclopædic character wearied him, and,
as he said to his friend, Max Müller, "it carried him
too far away from the vital questions of the age."

But in scarcely one of these " vital questions " was
he more interested than in the Abbey itself. To
commend its treasures to the public, to interest in its
monuments and walls, and services, every class of his
countrymen, soon became to him one of the most vital
of all questions. There is hardly a corner in the Abbey
on which he did not throw some new light: now pene-
trating underground till he had tracked the coffin of
the first Scottish King of England to its forgotten home
in the vault of Henry VII.; now placing in her husband's chantry the neglected remains of Catherine of
Valois; now carefully and reverently replacing the
recovered fragments of the desecrated tomb of the
young Protestant King, Edward VI. His hand and
spirit may be traced in the brightly tinted leaves of
an American autumn, that speak a message of reconciliation over the bones of André; in the monument,

with its characteristic inscription, erected to the two
Wesleys; in the faint reproduction of the sun shining
on Boston Harbour, which forms part of the memorial window which he raised to the memory of his lost
wife. It was his delight to take eminent strangers—
now a king, now a general, now a literary man, now a
party of children, now a listening friend, from tomb
to tomb; to answer their questions and pour out his
knowledge. Rarely did a Saturday pass in spring or
summer without his accompanying a party of working-men from end to end, through Jerusalem Cham-
ber, Chapter-House, and Abbey; often ending the
fatiguing task by giving them a simple meal, and
occasionally showing them the curiosities of the Deanery. In that ancient house of the Abbots of Westminster and earlier Deans he took the profoundest
interest. His malediction will fall, I am sure, on the
first of his successors who shall substitute modern
apartments for those antique gables and not wholly
commodious bed-rooms. The restoration of the Chapter-House, the cradle of English Parliamentary life,
inaugurated under his predecessor, was vigorously
urged on the Government and completed at last, all
but the windows. Every detail of the design for
these last was arranged by himself, and will be completed, in great part at least, as a fitting monument
to his memory. Had he never preached a sermon,
never published a line, never made a single speech,
never appeared in public on any general question, he
would have made his mark in those ancient precincts
as a memorable Dean.

For preaching too, and that from the most inspiring, to him, of all pulpits, he had now the ample scope that was grudged him at the University, and he was able to fulfil the promise which he had made in his parting sermon at Oxford. If to preach was, strictly speaking, his proper and official duty on three Sundays only in the year, yet the special circumstances of the Chapter gave him abundant opportunities; and Sunday after Sunday men and women, including many whom few preachers would have drawn to worship, crowded to hear him. If there were times, as must needs have been the case in one who preached so often and so readily, when the quality of his sermons fell in some respects below what had been looked for, yet the voice, the manner, the face, the tones, were something that could be found nowhere else, and at his best — in, for instance, such occasional sermons as he himself chose for publication, or such as are contained in a volume published since his death — he had for striking and moving eloquence few rivals in any English-speaking community of Christians. Read his funeral sermon on Charles Kingsley, on Sir John Herschel, on your own countryman Carlyle, or that preached on the Siege of Paris. Who else in the United Kingdom could have preached them? Read, indeed, any of his published sermons. We may say as Dr. Johnson said of Baxter's, " Read any; they are all good." Read any, we may add, for they are all characteristic, all stamped with his own impress. No one else in the world could have written them. I have

heard it said that it was worth a considerable journey
to hear him read in the Abbey certain lessons from the
New and even more from the Old Testament.   He had
a wonderful genius for finding in the services of the
day a happy and felicitous guide for the subject of his
sermon.   On a Sunday when the Shah of Persia was in
London, he had to preach to a regiment of volunteers.
His text was drawn from the Book of Esther, which
had formed for some days past the daily lessons.
The greatest personage in that book was "the very
last King of Persia who from that time to the present
had visited Europe," and the text was taken from
words of devoted patriotism — a very motto and watch-
word for citizen soldiers — uttered by Esther herself.

I have already spoken of his preaching on the re-
gathering of the brethren of Joseph which formed the
morning lesson on the Sunday after his hearing of his
mother's death; the text " *Abraham went down to
Egypt to sojourn there,*" he drew from the same
source for his first sermon in Egypt.   The same
dexterous readiness in catching analogies and simi
larities which gave such a charm to his conversa
tion, stood him also in good stead on very different
occasions.   In preaching, for instance, to the men
employed at the great Agricultural Show at Isling-
ton, he was able to find ennobling memories even for
the drovers of swine, if not in the associations of
Holy Scripture, yet in the faithful Gurth of Walter
Scott, and in the even more faithful Eumæus of the
" Odyssey."

But you in Scotland have heard him preach, and need no eulogies of mine.

You will now, perhaps, expect his successor to say something at greater length than he has yet said of his theological position. Yet what I have already said is the key to all that I could say. He stood aloof, absolutely aloof, from all parties in the Church. " I cannot," he said, in a letter to one of his dearest friends, " go out to battle in Saul's armour : I must fight with my own sling and stone or not at all. I have never been able to reconcile myself to these unreasoning, undiscriminating war-cries : whatever power I have been able to exert has been mainly derived from this abstinence."

Towards the close of his life, after quoting a famous passage on party spirit from Robert Hall, that opens with " Whatever retards a spirit of inquiry is favourable to error, whatever promotes it is favourable to truth," he added one of his favourite remarks : " This spirit of combination for party purposes, and this alone, is what the New Testament calls *heresy*, and this," he added, " constitutes the leading danger of synods and of councils."

Yet he was never ashamed of the title of " liberal theologian," not even " if he were to be the last who was to bear the name," and he was the first to give currency to the much used term " Broad Church." Liberal theology, he spoke of, in one of the very latest of his addresses, as being " the backbone of the Church of England," and he claimed for it an " or-

thodoxy, a biblical, evangelical, Catholic character
which its opponents have never reached."

What, you will ask, did he mean by this? I can
give you no better answer than in words of his own;
his theological views are repeated over and over again
with a monotony which is never monotonous in all
that ever came from his lips or pen.

Let me say first, that he was not, as you all know,
a lover of dogma. His dear friend, your countryman,
the Archbishop of Canterbury, said of him that "no
true believer in Christianity was ever more abhorrent
of dogmatism," and adds that " he was almost bigoted
against bigotry, and almost intolerant of intolerance."
But though this is quite true, I feel inclined to quote
some wise and discriminating words used by a much
respected writer in reference to his dear friend Hugh
Pearson, whose death soon followed his own, and who,
as I have already said, for over forty years had shared
every thought and feeling as none other of his friends:—

" There will probably always be two schools of
opinion respecting the true relations between Christian doctrine or dogma and Christian morals; the one
of those who think that the true spirit of the Gospel
has been fettered, if not perverted, by being too much
tied to doctrine, the other of those who believe that
in the careful custody of the faith, in every particular,
out of which Christian ethics sprang, is to be found
the only security for their permanent vitality and
power. The Vicar of Sonning " (let me substitute
the name of the Dean of Westminster) " unquestiona-

bly belonged to the former school. He had a devout
faith in the power and love of God, a profound reverence and love for Jesus Christ, and an absolute conviction that the truest wisdom and highest happiness
of man were to be found in the study and the imita-
tion of that holy, lovely, and beautiful life. This was
the sum and substance of his religion, this was really
the key-note of all his sermons. To this he turned
from doctrinal questions with something like con-
tempt, and some might think with too little consideration or perception of the bearing of such questions
upon the practical life. The whole condition of his
mind on this subject might be summed up in the
verses of Charles Wesley on Catholic Love : —

> ' Weary of all this wordy strife,
>   These notions, forms, and modes and names,
>   To Thee, the Way, the Truth, the Life,
>   Whose love my simple heart inflames —
>   Divinely taught at last I fly,
>   With Thee and Thine to live and die.' "

He was never, as you know, weary of repeating, 1st,
" that the essential superiority of Christianity to all
other religions in the world, lay in its resting on a
Divine life, a life that was the image of God, because
he who lived it was all goodness and truth " ; 2ndly,
" that its essential object was to produce characters
which in truthfulness, in independence, in mercy, in
purity, in charity, may recall something of the mind
that was in Christ " ; 3rdly, " that what makes a man a
Christian is to have the character of Christ," " a Mas-

ter worth living for, worth dying for, whose spirit was
to be the regenerating power of the whole world."

It is in the light of this intense feeling for goodness
and for truth as revealed in Christ, and presenting to
mankind a standard which system after system of
theology had only dimly realised — " as having far, far
more in it," as he delighted to say of the Bible, "than
has ever been taken out of it," — that we must view his
dissatisfaction with the imperfections of the past, "the
old theological Adam striving in each successive generation to maintain his own against the new Christian
spiritual Adam." Hence his reiterated claim to place
" all that was ceremonial, all that was dogmatic, even
all that was miraculous, on a lower level among the
essential elements of Christianity than what was moral
or spiritual." Hence his bold assertion "that the
greatest of all miracles is the character of Christ."
Hence his urgent advice to his American friends "to
feel truly the littleness of what is little, as well as the
greatness of what is great; to distinguish what is outward from what is inward, what is accidental from what
is essential, what is temporary from what is eternal."
Hence his fondness for the story of the French pastor
asking on his death-bed his friends " to pray for him
that he might have the elementary graces;" or of the
old Scottish Methodist, laying aside in his dying moments the narrow sympathies of his earlier years in
the words " if power were given me I would preach
purity of life more and purity of doctrine less." On
the realisation of this idea of a wider Christianity, "if

not in this century," as he said in America, "yet in
the next or in the next but one," "even if he were to be
the last not to despair of his religion and his Church,"
"even if a partial eclipse were at hand," — on this he
rested all his hopes of the triumph of faith over unbelief. At times, no doubt, his heart seemed to fail
him. "Those younger than himself might live," he
said, "to see a brighter and happier day than that
which seems to overcloud the minds, and oppress the
hopes, of those who live in the latter part of this nine-
teenth century." "The immediate future" seemed
to him "sometimes darkened by an eclipse of faith,
sometimes by an eclipse of reason." But he never
seriously relinquished the hope — call it, if you will,
an idle dream — that he expressed, as elsewhere, so
in Scotland, "that, in spite of cynical indifference or
growing superstition, it would yet be shown that
Christianity — a Catholic, comprehensive, all-embracing Christianity — was not dead or dying, but instinct with immortal life" — "that Christianity in its
wider aspect may yet overcome the world." It was to
this indestructible faith in the real vitality of what he
held to be "the essentials of Christianity," that we
may refer his impatience under all stringent subscriptions to church formularies and confessions of faith as
tending to alienate Christian from Christian, Church
from Church, and to retard the progress for which he
sighed. "All confessions and similar documents are,"
he said, "if taken as final expressions of absolute
truth, misleading," and he speaks of a church "whose
glory it is to be always advancing to perfection."

Truth he was ready to welcome from any quarter. It was in the firm conviction that " Truth was to be sought above all things for itself and not for any ulterior object," that he refused to be appalled at any discoveries, real or supposed, of physical science, but was ready to welcome all as elements of a larger system. " However far," he said, " we may trace back the material parts of man, from whatever earlier forms of existence it may be possible to derive the bodily frame which we possess in common with other parts of creation, no one can go further back or deeper down than St. Paul or the Book of Genesis have already led us. ' *The first man is of the earth earthy,*' says St. Paul ; ' *The Lord God made man of the dust of the earth,*' says the Book of Genesis. In neither the biblical nor the scientific account, can the description affect or destroy our knowledge, our certainty of what he is now. What would be fatal to our hopes, would be to be told, that because our first man was of the earth, earthy, therefore all our higher and nobler desires and hopes and affections are also of the earth, earthy. This would indeed make us, as St. Paul says, ' *of all creatures the most miserable.*' " And he protests against "driving into the devil's camp" all the leaders in such inquiries, just as he protests elsewhere against using, by way of disparagement, such words as "deist" or "theist," on the ground that "where this belief remains, the true supernatural, the true ideal, immaterial ground is not abandoned." Scotsmen know well how eager he was to find points

of agreement and similarity in dissident churches,
and the reproach of a late venerable Oxford Pro
fessor that "he had an eye for resemblances but not
for differences," he welcomed as the highest praise.
"Make the most," he said, in a sermon preached in
Old Grey Friars' Church, "of what there is of good
in institutions, in opinions, in communities, in indi-
viduals." He had, as you know, an avowed, a warm,
an almost passionate preference for the much decried
principle of an "Established Church," for the union,
wherever possible, of Church and State. He would
dwell, to the astonishment no doubt of conscientious
dissenters, "on the enlarging and elevating influence
infused into a religious institution by its contact,
however slight, with so magnificent an ordinance as
the British Commonwealth, by its having for its aim
the highest welfare of the whole community." "That
connection which Chalmers had vindicated in the
interest of Christian philanthropy, had," he said, "in
these latter days more and more commended itself
in the interest of Christian liberty." And he was
never tired of enlarging on the "soothing, moderat-
ing, comprehensive spirit of the Church of England."

Yet not the less he could thank the Baptists for
having "almost alone in the Western Church preserved intact one singular and interesting relic of primitive and apostolic times which we have," he adds,
"at least in our practice, wisely discarded." He
could point to their Bunyan, Robert Hall, and Have-
lock, as men who taught us that "there was a ground

of communion which no difference of external rites
could ever efface." He could thank Quakerism for
" having unfurled before the eyes of Christendom not
the flag of war but of peace;" for "dwelling even with
exaggerated force on the insignificance of all forms,
of all authority, as compared with the inward light
of conscience." "The work of dissenting churches
is," he said in Scotland, "to keep alive that peculiar
force of devotion and warmth which is apt to die
out in the light of reason, and in the breath of free
inquiry." "We cannot safely dispense," he said in
America, after a sermon full of wisdom on the characteristics of the Roman, the Eastern, the Lutheran,
and the Calvinistic systems, "even with the churches
which we most dislike, and which in other respects
have wrought most evil." If he felt that the absolute
and corporate re-union of Churches was in some
cases undesirable, in others impracticable, he did all
that lay in his power to advocate and to promote a
friendly inter-communion. You know how gladly he
preached in the pulpits of the Scottish Establishment,
how joyfully he would have opened to your own
clergy the pulpit of an· Abbey which he loved to call
" the consecrated temple of reconciled ecclesiastical
enmities," how in the absence of freedom fully to
effect this, he rejoiced to hear, if not in the pulpit,
yet beneath the roof of that Abbey, the voice of a
layman like Max Müller, of Scotsmen such as Prin-
cipals Caird and Tulloch, of such an English Nonconformist as Dr. Stoughton. How gladly did he dwell on

the manner in which men like Milton or John Bunyan,
or Thomas A'Kempis or Keble, or the writers of great
hymns, rise unconsciously above their own peculiar
views, "above the limits that divide denominations,
into the higher region of a common Christianity."
How he delighted in the words of your own Dr.
Chalmers, "who cares about any Church except as an
instrument of doing good?" or of Dr. Duncan, the
Free Church sage, who was "first a Christian, then
a Catholic, then a Calvinist, then a Pædo-Baptist,
and fifthly a Presbyterian," who avowed "that there
was a progress in all things and therefore in religion;"
who, though a staunch Protestant and disliker of
image worship, could never banish the touching memory of a rude image of his Saviour which he had seen
cut on a granite cross in Hungary. How he rejoiced
in the conviction of John Wesley's dearest friend
that "the main, fundamental, overpowering principle
of his life was not the promotion of any particular doctrine, but the elevation of the whole Christian world
in the great principles of Christian holiness and morality." How often has he quoted the words of Zwinglius, "of the meeting in the presence of God of every
blessed spirit, every holy character, every faithful soul
that has existed from the beginning of the world even
to the consummation thereof." His own words, as
applied to Richard Baxter, sum up all that under this
head can be said of himself: "In a stormy and divided
age he advocated unity and comprehension. Many other thoughts abounded in that teeming brain, but they

were more or less secondary. Other messages of divine
or human truth were delivered with more force and
consistency by others of his time, but in the solemn
proclamation of this message he stood pre-eminent."

You can imagine, or you know in part, how fierce a
spirit of opposition all this — and I have read you only
some fair specimens of his habitual teaching — must
have provoked in some minds. As those whose duty
it is to do so, read the fierce invectives, the malignant
insinuations which were launched against that noble
spirit, so full of the hunger and thirst after righteousness, so glowing with an all-embracing charity towards
every human soul, it is easy to repress what might
seem a natural, a righteous resentment. So clear is it,
if not on which side lies the victory in argument, or
the hope of immediate success, yet on which side is
the spirit of Christ. Let me give you, if you wish
for criticism — you will have none from me — something more worthy of himself. A lecture which he
once delivered is thus described by a member of the
Society of Friends, one who did not wholly share
his views, yet deeply sympathised with and greatly
reverenced him. " The subject was, 'The points in
the Christian creed which are held by all Christians.'
It was full of his own wonderful and all-embracing
charity, and he seemed to lift his whole audience into
a higher sphere as he spoke. The soul was soothed
and cheered by listening to him. Perhaps the intellect
was not altogether satisfied. If any man could have
succeeded in finding and describing the common stand-

ing ground of Roman Catholic and Unitarian, it would
have been he. But I think that one or two of us felt
that not even he had quite succeeded in finding that
common formula." Ah! how different this thoughtful
language to the taunts of some of his own communion.

" He spoke after his lecture," the same observer adds,
"of the manner in which ᛫ Ecce Homo ' had been received by the different sections of the Christian Church.
Each one had found something in the book which har-
monised with its own special views. This seemed to
him an illustration of the wonderful manifoldness of
our Lord's character, 'that character,' he said, 'which
is the foundation of the Church.'" His host adds an
interesting reminiscence of his speaking of the Founder of Buddhism. "I remember," said Stanley, " the
time when the ·name of Gautama was scarcely known,
except to a few scholars, and not always well spoken
of by those who knew it, and now — *he stands second.*"
" There was something," we are told, " very impressive in the way in which he said this — with hands
and eyes uplifted, leaving the name of the First un-
spoken." Those who knew him will easily fill up the
outlines of the picture.

You would wish me, I think, to say something of
the position which he held towards the working classes
in London, and in the nation generally. This also
was unique of its kind, and difficult at first sight
to define or account for. Other men have devoted
themselves far more exclusively and more assiduously
to promoting their welfare. Other men have spoken,

preached, and written in a style far more directly
adapted to their opinions and tastes. He had little, at
least in early life, of his father's frank, ready, sailor-like
power of at once placing himself on a level with less
educated strangers. He had never toiled and laboured
like his sister, Mary Stanley, in the details of hospital
life, or of organising industrial and other means of
relieving distress and encouraging self dependence.
It was not till he was established at Westminster
that he came into any specially close or permanent
contact with what are called the working classes.
While still at Oxford he had been deeply interested
in efforts made by his warm friends, Mr. Thomas
Hughes and the Rev. Septimus Hansard, under the
inspiration of Mr. Frederic Maurice, in conjunction
with the late Mr. Kingsley and others, to raise the
condition of the London operatives ; and it is needless
to say that, with Lady Augusta by his side, he gave the
aid of his presence and his sympathy to various move-
ments that tended to promote their welfare. Very soon
he won his way to their hearts, and was a welcome
visitor at their meetings. There remains at the Deanery an address presented to him by the working-men
of Westminster on his reaching his 60th birthday ; a
cheering memorial of their good wishes as the shadows
of life began to darken round him. He early formed
the habit, which he never laid aside, of conducting
Saturday parties of working-men round the Abbey,
explaining, as no one else could, the principal monuments, and endeavouring to interest them in the past

greatness of their common country, by trying, in language used by himself at his Installation sermon, "to
draw out the marvellous tale that lies imprisoned in
those dead stones, and make each sepulchre give up
again to life its illustrious dead." I have been favoured
with more than one description of such afternoons,
written by working-men who had been admitted to a
privilege which the most exalted personages delighted
to enjoy. In such tours of the Abbey or in the visits
to the Deanery that occasionally followed them were
laid, at times, the seeds of future intimacy with indi-
viduals. Yet I feel that these details throw but a faint
light on his relation to the men of whom I speak. It is
not the thing done — that is in the reach, if not of any
one yet of many — it is in the manner in which he did
it that the charm lay. I might easily enumerate other
claims to gratitude : his promotion of coffee-houses and
libraries, his hearty sympathy with the Working-Men's
Club and Institute Union, of which he was elected
President, his care to have every monument in the
Abbey carefully lettered and described; but I feel that
no list of such services will, in itself, account for the
place he held in the affections of his countrymen. The
truth was that the same sympathetic fibre, the same
indescribable gift for winning hearts, which was con-
stantly binding to him new friends among his own
class, and which made his death felt, in America as in
England, as a personal loss by multitudes who had
never seen him, told with no less force on a class not
often interested in the life and death of an ecclesiasti-

cal dignitary. Its effect was clearly marked when he
was laid in his grave. It was not only that the Abbey
and its approaches were thronged to the very full by
humble worshippers, or that in the meanest streets in
the neighbourhood there was scarcely a shop or a
public-house that was not partially closed as for a death
in the family, or that — as was said at the time by one
familiar with the purlieus of Westminster — "the hardest roughs seemed softened by his name." This might
have been in a measure due to years of ready beneficence and well-tried sympathy on the part of Lady
Augusta, his sister, and himself. But the feeling extended far beyond the vicinity of the Abbey. In a
great northern seat of industry, one who was coming
up from the Yorkshire Moors to bear his part in that
sad funeral, heard a working-man, as he put his son
into the train, bid him, in Yorkshire dialect, "tak care
of himself at the burying," and a few moments' conversation startled him by the interest shown in the loss
which was saddening his own heart. The same traveller spent the next two months in a Midland town,
where he made the acquaintance of some of the leading
operatives; and there, to his astonishment, he found
the name of Stanley, introduced in conversation by
men who were not aware that the new comer was his
friend, act at once as a passport to their confidence.
How was it? I must leave those who have felt the
spell of his presence, of his face, his voice, his greet-
ing, to add to these his reputation for chivalry and
courage and eloquence, and sympathy with all who

needed sympathy, and the wide-spread sense that he was the same man in the atmosphere of a court as at a meeting of working-men; that to use once more words quoted by himself but applied to another, "he feared no man's displeasure, and hoped for no man's preferment," and so to find a key to the un-doubted hold which that scion of an ancient family had won on the affection of the best representatives of our toiling millions.

I need not remind you how deeply, how univer-sally he was mourned. "He was borne to his grave," it was truly said, "on the shoulders of the nation." It may be no less truly said that the feelings which he inspired were a real force in breaking down, or at least softening, that alienation of classes which is the most formidable of all dangers to existing institu-tions. When the foremost men in England, the leaders in Parliament, in society, in science and literature, in church and state, met in the Chapter House of Westminster to do honour to his memory, no testimony was more impressive than that borne by one who represented neither high rank, nor political office, nor ecclesiastical dignity, but the working-men who mourned the loss not so much of a benefactor as of a friend. And they were not mistaken. If years before he had spoken in the distant East, in the pres-, ence of a circle far removed from their own, of God's love "to the poor, the humble classes, the neglected classes, the dangerous classes, the friendless, the op-pressed, the unthought for, the uncared for;" if he

had pleaded for Christianity "as the only religion
addressed, not to the religious, but to the irreligious,
the non-religious," his friends know well that this was
no rhetorical utterance of idle breath, but a deep conviction on which his own life and his own religion
were based and moulded.

The many volumes of his collected works will have
to face the verdict which it is yet too early to pronounce
as to their enduring character. His theological position
may be questioned, challenged, attacked, and defend-
ed; it may be maintained or abandoned by those who
survive him. But those who have had the privilege—
the inestimable privilege — of enjoying his society or
of sharing his friendship, will feel that behind the
genius and behind the theology there was something
more precious, more attractive, more inspiring than
either; the man himself — the Arthur Stanley — who
in youth, in manhood, in maturer age, drew to him
more and more the hearts of men, and has made the
skies seem less bright, earth less habitable, life itself
less interesting since he ceased to be.

I would gladly end with these words: but something I ought to say of his domestic, his personal
history. You will not expect me to anticipate his
biography by saying much.

His life was exceedingly busy and laborious. He
speaks frequently in letters written on his first coming
to London of "the terrible whirl," of "my time being
broken to pieces in useless, trivial labour." His successor can enter into his dismay. Yet the amount of

work — work of the most various kinds — which he contrived to do seems almost incredible. And he did it in the main joyously. No controversialist's abuse ever seemed to ruffle him for a moment; the fiercest invectives left no sting behind. His health, without being strong, was good, and his autumnal tours in Scotland, or on the Continent, he enjoyed to the last with indefatigable activity. The loss of friends he felt sorely. Kingsley's death struck him to the ground. So wide was his circle that such blows came often as life went on. "I am thankful now," he said, "if a month passes without a death!" Yet he had wonderful elasticity and a hopeful temperament. I remember his telling us how, near the time of his sixtieth birthday, a little German boy with whom, with his usual love of children, he had made acquaintance (I think it was on a Rhine steamer), asked him his age; on hearing it, he said, "Why, all your life is over!" "No," he replied, "the best time is yet to come." He took a keen interest in public affairs, and was deeply moved by the war between France and Germany. His letters express the strongest indignation against the French Emperor as the wanton disturber of the peace of Europe. But the bombardment of Strasburg and the siege of Paris were to him "dreadful calamities, even if needed to secure the world against the recurrence of such evils." And in his sermon on the Distress of Paris you will find the most moving of laments over the city which he knew so well. But I must hasten on.

It was after his visit to Russia in 1874 that his wife's

health began to show signs of failure, and that sadness
began to darken that once bright home in the Deanery.
In the next year it was necessary to pass the spring and
summer in seclusion, and to forego their usual visit to
Scotland.   He writes of his "suffering wife and her
widowed sister as cheering each other and cheering
me."   "I resign myself," he says, "to six months of
this stranded existence.   If at the end of that time
my dear wife is anything like what she was before in
activity and strength, I shall be satisfied.   Like what
she was in wisdom and goodness she is and has been
throughout, and will be, I have no doubt, to the end."
(To M. M., Feb. 8, 1875.)   He spent the autumn at
Norwood near London, busying himself, seated by her
couch-side, at his third volume of the Jewish Church,
in alternations of hope and despondency.   He returned
to London in October.   But the months went by, and
no change for the better came.   "I know not," he
writes to the same friend, "what report to give. So very
weak, so suffering, and yet such unconquerable cheerfulness and vivacity."   And he speaks of the invaluable
presence of her cousin, that most faithful of friends,
who is even now devoting herself to the sacred task
of deciphering and arranging a vast mass of his letters,
papers, and journals.   "All the world is changed for
me," he adds; "yet I find it best, and she also desired,
that I should fill up the time, not filled by my thoughts
and works for her, with work of my own, and so I
struggled on."   And through that sad winter, ever ready
to forget his own trouble if he could aid a friend or

further any good cause, he worked day by day at that concluding volume. By February she could only just rouse herself to express her joy that her husband and Oxford were not to lose the presence of so dear a friend as Professor Max Müller. Still he worked on by her side, placing, when speech had failed her, some simple hymn, some Christian text, within her sight. "Last night," he writes at last to his old pupil and present successor, "she pronounced my name for the last time; this morning, for the last time, in answer to my urgent appeal, she opened those dear eyes upon me." On the 1st of March she passed away. The last visitor to look upon her as she lay in the calm of unconscious slumber was the Sovereign's youngest son, the young Prince dear to Scotland for other reasons than the Scottish title that he bears, whose recovery from dangerous illness twelve months before he had made the subject of some touching lines, under the title of "The Untravelled Traveller," which some here may have read.* It was Ash-Wednesday —the same day of the ecclesiastical year as that on which he had lost his mother fourteen years before. Something of his feelings towards both he embodied in stanzas of characteristic and mournful beauty to which I have already referred.†

He was, indeed, "in the very ashes and embers." Yet the sympathy of his friends, the letters that poured in upon him from every quarter of the world, cheered him greatly. "The knowledge," he wrote once more,

---

* Macmillan's Magazine, March 1875.   † See note to page 89.

"that my friends, my dear unfailing friends, knew what she was and is, must be my enduring solace." " Do not pity me for Thursday " (the day fixed for the funeral). " What could be more sustaining and inspiring than such a tribute rendered to the life of my life, the heart of my heart ? " Some here may possibly have been present at that vast gathering—second only in impressiveness to another that we have since seen moving towards the same tomb—which walked behind him to her grave. How anxiously, during the long roll of a music into whose secrets he could not enter, men watched his face as he stood sustained and calm behind the coffin. With what courage, what almost majesty, he himself, before he returned to his darkened home, dismissed with the final blessing that vast multitude, awed, thrilled, and touched by the strange power and resonance of that unfaltering voice—a multitude that included every class, from the Queen who loved her to the poor workers for their daily bread whose lives she had helped to cheer.

But the blow had been struck from which he was never wholly to recover. He often loved to speak of lives which great affliction had strengthened and elevated. He would point with admiration to that sorely-tried friend the Primate of England, who had gathered strength and renewed usefulness from crushing sorrows. There is an exquisite passage in one of his latest sermons in which, after speaking of "the blank desolation of sorrow with which we look on the lonely work that lies before us when the voice that cheered us is silent,

and the hand that upheld us is cold in the grave," he
speaks also of "the cloud of blessing that comes out of
that tender memory, and of the feeling that the very
solitude in which we are left calls for new energies."

Two months after his bereavement he laments that
it is not so with himself. "Sorrow has not yet brought,"
he writes, "strength and energy. I still hope that it
will." And his hope was not wholly in vain. Care was
taken that his home should be never wholly desolate.
He lived, as you know, for five years longer. Old
friends rallied round him; new friendships were still to
be formed. One who for those last few years saw him
almost daily, and who repaid his warm affection by
a devoted and almost filial attachment, had never
known him in his married life. He recovered his full
interest in public events, in the questions which agi-
tated the Church. He worked on at the same desk in
the library, with his wife's bust hard by on the table
by which she had sat. Much of his old elasticity and
vivacity returned; his keen sense of humour never left
him. He was as ready as ever to take the field in
defence of any victim of theological prejudice or ran-
cour. His interest in his humbler fellow-countrymen
grew deeper and wider. There lies before me at this
moment a letter from one of the mourners who filled the
Abbey at his funeral. It is written by a London lighter-
man, *i.e.*, a navigator of barges on the Thames, whom
he had accidentally encountered in front of the monument to John Wesley on the Easter Monday of the
year before he died. Their chance conversation had led

to two or three friendly visits paid by invitation to the
Deanery. The humbler friend recalls not only his own
remark, in reference to the Dean's visits to Palestine,
that it must " have been beautiful to have been able
to walk where the Saviour had walked," but the
answer and " the heavenly look " that came with it,
" Yes, beautiful to walk in the steps of the Saviour."
And his visitor and others like him learned to look on
him with the same love that we his old familiar friends
bore to him. Of work he had no lack, and he never
rested from work except in such rest as travel brought
him. He seemed to find a new lease of life, for a time
at least, in his visit made to America with two dear
friends in 1878. There he renewed many friendships,
formed fresh ties, and drank in with delight the throng
of new ideas which pressed upon him in his first visit
to that untrodden region. If the volume of " Addresses and Sermons in America " were the only relic
left of his literary labours, if all else from the Biography of Arnold to the " Christian Institutions "
were swept away, you might find in that one volume
almost everything characteristic of the man, and
some gems of a kind not to be found in his earlier
writings. To these I have referred elsewhere.

At the meeting which was held to take steps to
commemorate him in the Chapter House of Westminster, the Archbishop of Canterbury told a touching story of a poor old widow at Lambeth whose
face brightened up on hearing his name. " Frail and
trembling," she said, " I was trying to make my way

across Westminster Bridge among the carriages, and
afraid that I should be trodden down, when a man
stepped up to me and gave me his help, and piloted
me safely through the crowd.   I asked him to whom
I was indebted; he merely pointed to the great Abbey, ' You know that place,' he said ; ' I am its Dean.' "

Let me add another characteristic anecdote.   In his
absence from home for some weeks, a much respected
servant of the Abbey, a man of humble position, but
rich in health and strength, and vigour and stature,
had become permanently and hopelessly blind.   My
informant, his one surviving sister — none but herself
could have told the tale so touchingly — found him
seated by the side of the blind man, his own eyes
streaming with tears, which he whom he was trying to
comfort could not see, endeavouring by every possible
word and topic to inspire hope and courage into the
heart of one who was visited with what would have
been to himself the most terrible of afflictions.   No
wonder that the sufferer found his burden lightened
by the aid of such a friend, and was encouraged to
take the first and hardest steps towards leading, in
spite of that great loss, a cheerful and useful life.

From America he returned to his work refreshed and
strengthened for a time.   But there was a sense among
those who knew him best that his hold on life was
slackening.   Yet his busy brain never rested, nor did
the warm heart grow cold.   It was only shortly before
his death that he published the volume on Christian
Institutions," which embodies his latest views on the

whole field of Theology. The exquisite lines on "Death
the Reuniter," were written not long before death did
its kindly work. His sermon on Thomas Carlyle was
preached in the February before the preacher died;
that on Lord Beaconsfield so late as the 1st of May.
Within a few weeks of the end he wrote for *The Times*
a paper which appeared after his death on the revised
version of the New Testament; an article on the
Westminster Confession he corrected for the Press,
on what proved to be his death-bed. In the year
but one before he died he had greatly enjoyed a visit
to Northern Italy and Venice in company with his
sister, Mary Stanley, and a young London physician,
whom he greatly loved, and who had been one of his
two companions in America. It was followed, in November, by that sister's death, coming, if it must needs
have come, even as they would both have wished it,
yet for all that a sore trial. The last but one gone of
that bright circle! Father, mother, brothers, sister,
gone before him!

Shall I remind you of the one storm of popular,
as opposed to clerical, opposition that he ever encountered? His own words will recall it. "When,"
he said, "I assented to a monument in the Abbey
to the Prince Imperial, I expected, after the sympathy shewn at the time of the funeral at Chisle-
hurst, nothing but universal approval. I did it without consulting or hearing from any one, and I still
believe that a few years hence it would have been
amongst the most generally interesting and attractive

of the Abbey monuments." Yet he was no Napoleon-
ist, and had little sympathy for either the First or
the Second Empire. His intended inscription for the
proposed monument, was the untranslatable line of
Virgil, —

"Sunt lacrimæ rerum et mentem mortalia tangunt."

He asked a friend to suggest a corresponding English
quotation. He demurred to Wordsworth's lines,

"Men are we, and must grieve when e'en the shade
Of that which once was great has passed away,"

as expressing a certain excess of homage to what had
fallen, and seemed more ready to acquiesce in the
vaguer words of the same poet,

"Yet tears to human sufferings are due."

The result of a debate in the House of Commons
seemed to him sufficient grounds for abandoning the
projected memorial; but he never changed his opinion, or was for a moment dismayed by the storm that
arose. "He feared no·man's displeasure."

Let me hasten onwards. In the year before his
death, his friends had been made uneasy by occasional
failures in strength; but he seemed in the last few
months to have recovered in no small degree his wonted
tone, and preached, if often with less than the usual
vigour, yet at times with all his old force and fire. But
the lamp of life was burning low. "I shall never go
again," he said, after his return from the triennial
dinner of Old Rugbeians; "I do not mean that I shall
not live, but I feel that I am losing interest in these

special and youthful meetings." Something of the same
kind he had whispered on his last return from Oxford.
This was within a fortnight of the commencement of
his last illness. The next day, however, he shewed the
keenest interest in an account given him by a young
Scottish friend of the feelings and language of a London
mob who were met together in support of Mr. Brad-
laugh. So anxious was he to the very last—it was the
last time I saw him—to find, if possible, some germ of
good in what most revolted the educated and religious
classes. A few days later he attended for some hours
the annual gathering within the Abbey precincts of the
Westminster Window Garden Exhibition, presided
over by the venerable Lord Shaftesbury, a meeting in
which he had for many years taken the deepest interest.

But the end was at hand. On the following Saturday he closed the afternoon service with a short
sermon, one of a course which he was delivering
weekly on the Beatitudes. Before the Psalms of the
day were ended he had left the Abbey, feeling ill;
he returned exhausted with violent sickness, and
preached his last sermon with an effort which few
but himself would have faced. For the first time in
his life at Westminster he was compelled to disap-
point a party — I believe of young sailors — who
were expecting his guidance round the Abbey.

He retired to bed on his return to the Deanery, and
except for a short time on the following Wednesday
never left it till, after two or three days of graver ill-

ness, he passed away towards midnight on Monday, the 18th of July.

You will not ask me to enter further into these sad details. Some of those closest and dearest to him were far away, unaware of his danger till all was over. But his dear friend, the Archbishop of Canterbury, came to his bedside, and took from him, before he left, his dying words; his one remaining sister and her husband, his wife's sister, his two fellow-travellers in America,—both exceedingly dear to him,—and his friend and neighbour Canon Farrar, were with him to the end, and all received, before utterance failed him, his parting blessing.

Shall I do wrong in passing from that solemn scene to language used not long before by himself, when speaking of the wrestling of Jacob with his mysterious visitor as the likeness and type of all spiritual struggles? "It describes also the last struggle of all, it may be in the extreme of age or of weakness, in the Valley of the Shadow of Death. There the soul finds itself alone on the mountain ridge overlooking the unknown future; 'our company before is gone,' the kinsfolk and friends of many years are passed over the dark river, and we are left alone with God. We know not in the shadow of the night who it is that touches us — we feel only that the Everlasting arms are closing us in; the twilight of the morning breaks, we are bid to depart in peace, for by a strength not our own we have prevailed, and the path is made clear before us."

Let me only add the closing lines of the same paper,

" When the struggle is drawing to its end, when the
day breaks and the sun rises, there will have been some
who in that struggle have seen the Face of God."

To him the night was past, and the daybreak had
dawned.